DISCOVERING PRIDE

JILL SANDERS

GRAYTON

This is a work of fiction. Names, characters, places and incidents either are the product of the author's imagination or are used fictitiously, and any resemblance to actual persons, living or dead, business establishments, events or locales is entirely coincidental.

DISCOVERING PRIDE

ISBN: 978-1-942896-08-1

Copyright © 2012 Jill Sanders

Edited by Erica Ellis – http://ericaellisfreelance.com

*To the three special men in my life, who have
been there with an eager ear to listen to a tale.*

&

*For the many dogs that have come and gone,
always there with a wag in their tails,
slobbery kisses, and undying love.
Let's play ball.*

SUMMARY

Lacey Jordan is a woman who knows what she wants…and she wants nothing to do with the new doctor in town. He has a perfect smile, perfectly tan muscles, and a way with people —her people! This is her town, her family, and her life, and he's come here shaking everything up, including her heart.

Aaron is running away from a tough breakup where heartbreak is the least of his concerns. All he wants now is to take over his grandfather's medical practice and make his new house a place he can call home. What he hadn't counted on was crashing into a petite goddess with relentless powers of persuasion. When the two get a disturbing visit that could change their lives forever, Aaron must prove his love if they are to survive.

CHAPTER 1

*A*cool breeze drifted over the tall trees, floating down towards the still waters of a large pond, causing the lily pads to stir. Dragonflies buzzed from flower to flower, and frogs hopped along the grassy shore.

Every now and then, a lone leaf would break free from a branch and float slowly down to the moss-covered forest floor. Soon it will be winter, and this little piece of heaven will be covered in snow. All the insects and animals will be tucked away for the cold days and nights. But today the pond waters were buzzing with life.

Lacey Jordan was a free-spirited woman who enjoyed the fresh air, blue skies, and nature sounds that surrounded her home in Pride, Oregon. Even though summer was ending, the fall temperatures had reached a record high. A true Indian summer was in full swing.

Lacey was happily floating alone in the pond that bordered her property. Well, she wasn't quite alone; Bernard had been running in and out of the water, digging in the mud near the shore. Bernard was Lacey's first love, and to date, her only. He was everything she wanted in a man; loyal, loving, brave, and a great listener. Not to mention he was blonde, brown eyed, and loved to snuggle. His only faults were that he hogged the bed, slobbered a lot, and was extremely hairy, but no one was perfect.

Bernard was Lacey's three-and-a-half-year-old Labrador Retriever.

As she floated in the water, her short black hair bobbed around her face, a face often described as pixie-like. Her straight nose was, in her opinion, her best asset, but most people claimed it was her crystal slate eyes that stood out the most. An artist who had once painted her, compared her to an exotic creature from beyond this world.

A small crease formed between her eyebrows at the thought of being compared to an exotic or even mythical creature. It happened often and she was getting tired of it. To her, she was just Lacey, a down-to-earth woman in her mid-twenties whom, at this point, had yet to fall in love.

Most people in her town knew she had an uncanny way of predicting what was going to happen. Sometimes it seemed like she could even control the outcome. However, she felt that she just paid attention to everything more than others normally did.

Today she didn't want to think of the town or it's inhabitants. She forced herself to relax again as she studied the bright clear sky through the blanket of leaves on the trees overhead. Today she was going to enjoy her favorite place, the pond, which was in the woods between her house and her brother, Todd's house.

Every once in a while, Bernard would swim out to check on her or bark to make sure his presence was still known. She could spend hours out here, lost in thought, which would sometimes make her late for work. She was grateful she wasn't expected anywhere today so she could continue floating and relaxing as she pleased.

Lacey had been born and raised in Pride, and this was home. There had been a time when she'd craved travel, wanting to expand her horizons and become a woman of the world. However, after spending over a year traveling around Europe, she had needed to be home again. She missed taking walks along the beach or sitting in front of a fire with her father and brothers. She had made it home only to lose her father and she struggled through her loss. Her family needed her close and she needed them in return.

She started treading water as she remembered the weeks after she had come home. It had been some of the hardest times for the Jordan family, learning to adjust to the changes after the accident that had claimed their father's life and left their brother Iian battered and without his hearing. But the family had conquered a lot together, learning sign language and running the family businesses. They had learned to take care of each other.

Looking up, she saw Bernard happily running around the shore chasing the ducks that kept trying to land.

AARON STEVENS WAS RESTLESS, hot, and sweaty. And he was horny. His *need* reminded him it had been over seven months since his breakup with Jennifer. He'd spent the last few days hammering away on his house, spending all his pent-up anger and hurt on demolition. Now, however, he was still hot, angry, sweaty, and horny.

When he had purchased the old house, he'd known it needed a lot of work. But he'd thought the project would help him keep his mind off the fact that he'd almost made the biggest mistake of his life. He had learned a valuable lesson in love, and it had only cost him his heart.

When he hit his thumb for the tenth time in the last half

hour, he threw the hammer across the room. But because there were no walls in the place, it flew across the room and hit the floor with a dull thud, giving him no satisfaction.

The first thing he'd done was rip up the bright orange carpet, and now the entire house echoed. He had plans for hardwood or tile in the place, but he had yet to decide on which. All he knew was that the carpet had to go.

He stalked from the room, fuming and frustrated, his thumb throbbing like a bitch. When he reached the back door, he kept on going.

Soon he found himself on a path in a part of the woods he hadn't explored yet. There was a fork in the path, one that lead to his closest neighbors, Megan and Todd Jordan. They had been his first patients after taking over his grandfather's medical practice.

He paused by the head of the path and remembered walking into the hospital room after Megan had been rescued from her crazy ex-husband.

Megan had seemed so small and pale, bruised by the whole ordeal, but she and Todd's unborn child had survived. Her ex-husband, Derek, was now on trial for the murder of a federal guard. Todd had hovered over her and protecting her, which gained him instant respect in Aaron's book.

Aaron had done an ultrasound at the hospital, printing as many pictures as Todd had wanted. He felt compassion for the new family. He could tell they had a rough start but knew they would turn out okay. The pregnant mother had been fine, and he had seen them again just yesterday for another checkup.

Aaron was almost to a clearing before he heard the dog barking. He was so deep in his thoughts, he hadn't realized how far and which direction his wandering had taken him. Was he still on his property?

Just then, a wet yellow lab came running down the path

towards him. The dog wagged its tail. Aaron held out his hand for it to smell as it ran up; the dog sniffed his hand, then licking it. The entire time it's tail was wagging at full speed, then quickly turned and ran off in the opposite direction.

Smiling after the animal, Aaron continued down the path. He came to a clearing with a good size pond in the middle of tall grass. The water looked calm and cool, so he decided to cool off before heading back to the house and hammer.

Tossing off his clothing quickly, he dove from a huge flat rock that hung over the water's edge. Cutting deep through the cool crisp water, he was halfway across the small pond when his body hit something solid—solid, but definitely soft. He reached up and getting a hand full of soft skin, pushed up from the muddy bottom.

LACEY HEARD Bernard run off down the path, barking. Thinking he was probably chasing a bird, she dove under the water one last time. She wanted to stop by Megan's later to see how she and the baby were doing. Maybe she would even make them dinner.

When she was in the middle of the pond, she bumped into something solid. Then she was grabbed and pulled upwards by warm hands.

When Aaron surfaced he heard the sexiest voice he'd had the pleasure of hearing.

"What do you think you're doing?" she sputtered after surfacing, shaking her head to clear it.

His hands were holding the struggling creature and she was soft, small, and naked. Her hair was short, silky black, and it was slicked back from her face—a beautiful face at that. Her eyes were silver and seemed to penetrate into him and she had a cute little nose that sloped up at the end. There was a very small dimple in her chin and her lips were full and puckered ever so slightly. She had a look on her face that told him this was her pond and he was the intruder here.

"What do we have here?" Aaron said holding the squirming woman. She looked like a drenched pixie as he smiled down at her.

"You can take your filthy hands off me." Lacey pushed against his chest, but he didn't budge. Shaking the water from her eyes, she got her first look at him.

He looked like a Greek god, his hair a mass of dripping, golden blonde locks; that were a little longer than her own. His skin was golden, and his eyes were a deep rich brown, and he had a strong firm chin. His body was tight against her own and it was warm, firm, and naked. She pushed harder against his chest, but again he didn't budge.

"Hmm, I don't think that my hands are dirty any longer," he said with a slow smile. He kicked his legs a few times making sure their heads stayed above the water. He felt her legs against his; they were soft and smooth, making him want to tangle in them. He could see her chest rising and falling with each breath she took. The water lapped lower on the most perfect pair of breast he'd had the pleasure of seeing in his almost thirty years. She tried to push him away again, but he pulled her closer, until he could feel her cool skin against his burning skin.

"Let's see what happens when I..." He lowered his head, intending on tasting.

When his head started descending towards her mouth, she panicked. "Let me go before I scream," she whispered in a shaky tone.

He heard the panic in her voice. Pulling his head away, he looked into her eyes and he could see the panic there.

Lacey felt his muscular hairy legs against hers and she

could see a light coat of blonde hair on his tan chest. A chest, she noted, which was full of toned rippling muscles.

Shaking his head to clear it, he pulled away from her just as she reached up and pushed his head under the water. He stayed under for a moment, allowing his mind to cool.

In that moment, he saw her duck under the water. She quickly ran her eyes over him, turned her back and swam towards the shore at a speed that impressed him.

He drifted under the water for another few seconds, trying to clear his head. When he pushed himself up, he shook the water from his eyes and looked towards the shore. He didn't see anyone. Where had she disappeared to? He glanced around, but she was nowhere to be found. How could she have disappeared so quickly? There were some bushes and a rock to the left, but nothing big enough to conceal a woman. Turning in circles, he scanned the entire area, looking for any movement. Nothing!

Was he going crazy? What was he doing? Had she even really existed? Had he imagined her? No!

He could still feel the warmth from her breath on his face, and when he closed his eyes he could smell her. Dunking his head under the water again, he looked around the pond. From what he could see, he was the only inhabitant. Pushing up again, he scanned one more time and then finally called out.

"Hello?" Nothing!

He must have been hornier then he'd thought to imagine a sexy water pixie. Shaking his head, he decided he could use a few laps to cool his libido.

CHAPTER 2

*L*acey lay down in the grass breathing quietly. She could hear him swimming around. When he had called out, she had known her hiding spot was safe. Not wanting to draw any attention to herself, she stayed where she was, until she heard him swim ashore. Then curiosity got the better of her, and she rolled over to her stomach and pushed aside some tall grass to take a peek.

His back side was even better than his front. When she had ducked down to escape him, she had taken in his whole body – tan, muscular, and hard. She had almost swallowed a mouth full of water. Now as he reached over and picked up his discarded jeans she took in his tight butt. Wow. She slowly let out a soft breath.

Who was he? Where did he come from? Was he a guest at Megan's bed and breakfast? What was he doing in her pond? And, she thought, how did he get such a tight butt?

When he had disappeared down one of the paths, she rolled over and quickly grabbed her clothing, which had been hanging over a low branch behind a bush.

Once dressed, she jogged down the path heading towards

her own house. Hitting the house at a run, she skidded to a halt when she reached the front porch and saw Bernard curled up on the door mat.

"What kind of protector are you?" She bent down and scratched his head. When he rolled over, she said, "Oh no, no belly rubbing until you earn it."

Bernard followed her into the house, and she decided to head over to Megan and Todd's early for dinner. She was in the mood to cook but cooking for one was no fun.

She had been the only woman in a house full of men, so she learned early how to run a household. She practically raised her brother, Iian, who had never known life with a mother because theirs had died delivering him.

Todd was the oldest by several years and had married his high school sweetheart at a young age. But tragedy had struck when she died, and Todd had moved back into the house that stood on the cliff.

That is when Todd had started helping their father with the family company, Jordan Shipping. When their father had perished a few years later, Todd had taken control of the business altogether, while Lacey and Iian watched over the family's other business, a restaurant, which had been in their family for generations. It was more to their pace.

While Iian ran the kitchen, Lacey enjoyed running the restaurant; she had a good head for business.

She had always wanted a sister and since Todd and Megan's wedding a few weeks ago, she not only gained a sister, but a niece or nephew was now on the way.

As she headed upstairs to her room for a shower; she met Iian on the stair landing. They had the same jet-black hair even though Lacey's was shorter than his at the moment. They also had the same silver blue eyes and small but prominent dimple on their chins.

Where Lacey stood only five-foot-four inches, Iian and

Todd were both well over six feet tall. Her father had always said she took after her mother. She could scarcely remember her mother other than sometimes recalling a soft voice or warm arms rocking her to sleep.

Using sign language, she asked Iian if he was heading to work.

He kissed her cheek and answered, "Yes, running late. See you, sis." She watched him disappear down the stairs and out the front door.

She was worried about her brother. He'd been spending way too many hours at the restaurant. She was sure he still went in even on his nights off. Even though they owned the place, they both made a point to work only five nights a week. However, Iian had been going into town every night for the last several months. Did he have a girl? She didn't think he'd been seeing anyone seriously, not since the accident that claimed his hearing.

She shook her head as she headed up to take a shower. She looked around her big room as she undressed; this had always been her room. It was huge with bay windows that overlooked the yard and the ocean. Looking around, she realized how big it truly was. One wall was covered with mirrors and her barre, remnants from when she had the urge as a young child to become a ballerina. Her father and oldest brother had quickly put them up at her request. She still used them, every once in a while, to help her with her yoga.

The walls of the room were still painted a deep pink from yet another request as a teenager. She supposed that her room really did reflect her childhood personality. Now, looking around, she realized she had somewhat outgrown everything in the room. Gone was the child who wanted pink walls, ballet barres, and canopy beds high up in her own castle.

Stepping into her bathroom and the shower, her mind

played over the scene at the pond. It had been the closest she'd ever gotten to a naked man. She had truly been sheltered growing up. Her brothers had always protected her by keeping the boys at bay. But now she was almost twenty-five, she could make up her own mind about the men she did or didn't see in her life. After what she'd seen at the pond, she knew she wanted to see more of the blonde man who swam naked in someone else's pond.

An hour later, she was still distracted by her thoughts as she walked towards Megan and Todd's place. Bernard was on her heels, no doubt hoping for some tummy rubs and leftovers.

AARON HAD BEEN INVITED to Todd and Megan's for dinner. They were fast becoming some of his favorite people in the small town. He had walked over to their house using the short path from his place several times now. He had even journeyed to the beach past the cottages they rented out as part of their bed and breakfast business.

He'd just reached the edge of the clearing at the back of the big house when he saw movement out of the corner of his eye. He rubbed his eyes to make sure the image didn't disappear this time. He stood in the middle of the path and watched the water pixie walk right towards the house. Her head was lowered as she spoke to the dog that walked beside her.

She wore a white flowing sun dress, the color of snow. Her shoulders were bare, and he saw with great pleasure that her back was almost fully exposed. He watched her float out of the forest and up the back steps into the house without knocking.

When she disappeared inside, the yellow dog he'd met

earlier on the path laid down on the back steps in front of the door. Aaron continued towards the house with a wide smile on his face.

———

WHEN LACEY WALKED into the house, she found Megan and Todd in the kitchen, kissing. They must not have heard her, so she coughed softly, and they slowly pulled away from one another. Todd kept his arms lightly around his new bride.

The kitchen was one of Lacey's favorite rooms in this house. It was old fashioned, but with newer appliances, thanks to Matt, Megan's brother, who had redecorated it shortly after moving in. He'd chosen nice light colors, making the room feel like spring every day of the year. Lacey loved cooking, but she really enjoyed it more in someone else's kitchen.

"How are my favorite people today?" she asked, making herself at home. Then she noticed that Todd had cooked a larger meal. Pots and pans simmered on the stove, and the place smelled of good food.

Her family had become accustomed to treating this house as home when Matt had lived here. They continued to do so now that Megan and Todd called it home since Matt's death.

"We are doing great." Todd walked over and gave her a kiss on the cheek.

From outside, Bernard let out a happy bark and then there was a knock on the door.

"Oh, I forgot," Megan said with a smile. "We invited Dr. Stevens for dinner."

"Oh, good, it'll be nice to see..." Lacey's words stopped short when Todd opened the back door. The man from the pond was walking in, instead of the hundred-year-old doctor that Lacey had grown up with.

"What are you doing here?" Lacey asked taking two full steps backwards and bumping into the stove.

Aaron walked in and shook Todd's outstretched hand. He sent Lacey a quick smile across the room. "Good evening," he said to Todd. "Thank you for inviting me."

Slightly concerned, Todd turned towards Lacey and said, "Lacey, this is Dr. Steven's grandson, Aaron. Now that his grandfather has retired, he is our new doctor. Aaron, this is my sister Lacey."

Lacey remembered now, of course she had heard about him, the news had been all over town.

Aaron walked towards Lacey. "It's a pleasure to meet you." He held out his hand, and with satisfaction he saw her hands dart behind her back right before she slowly reached out to take his own in a shaky handshake.

He held her hand in his and felt the warmth from her soft skin. Lingering far more than he should have, he enjoyed seeing her eyes fire up and her cheeks heat.

Lacey tugged her hand free and put it behind her back again, trying to not look guilty. She hadn't done anything that would make her feel ashamed. It was, after all, her private swimming hole. She grew up swimming in it every summer. It was Aaron who should be feeling guilty. After all, who was he to jump naked in her pond?

AARON TOOK a good look at her; she was smaller than he'd first thought. Her head was below his shoulders, and with her tiny frame she looked very delicate.

"I purchased the Bell's house just down the way," he smiled. "I'm rebuilding it, which is hard work, and it's hot. That pond of yours was sure nice and cool today, just what the doctor ordered." He gave her a smile and winked at her, clearly telling her what he meant.

"Oh, you found the pond, did you? It really isn't ours. I guess it borders all three properties," Todd said.

"Megan, you're looking better." Lacey changed the subject quickly. She was sure her face was turning beet red. Was it getting hotter in the room, or was it just her?

"I feel a lot better, I'm glad the morning sickness is over. Now I just get tired early in the evenings," she smiled. "Todd, why don't you and Aaron go set the table in the dining room? Lacey and I will finish up in here and bring dinner out."

"Sure, come on into the den," Todd said, walking out with Aaron behind him.

When the men left the room, Megan turned on Lacey. "Okay, what was that all about?"

"Please, please, just shoot me." Lacey sat down at the table and put her head down on the cool wood. "This afternoon, I was taking my normal swim at the pond, and well... bumped into him. I guess he had the same idea of how to cool off as I did."

Megan smiled down at the back of Lacey's head. Todd and she had gone swimming in the pond a few nights ago themselves to "cool off". She knew how they had swam and imagined Lacey and Aaron had been swimming the same way—naked.

Megan sat down on a chair and a small laugh escape her lips. "Oh, that is rich. Tell me all the details," she said leaning forward over her small, but growing belly.

Lacey looked up and for a second time her face flushed. Then she leaned in and told her friend and sister every detail.

DINNER WAS different from anything Aaron had ever experienced. These people actually talked to each other and laughed while enjoying their meal. He was sucked into feeling like he was part of their family. At one point, he was laughing so hard he thought he might choke on the meatloaf.

Growing up, his parents had been too wrapped up in their careers and wealth to raise him themselves. Most of his childhood had been spent in boarding schools, and teachers had been his only authority figures. His only true enjoyment, when he'd been young, was the two weeks that he spent visiting his grandfather's house in Pride every other summer.

During dinner, Lacey had caught Aaron staring at her several times and by the end of the evening she was a ball of nerves. Her anxiety increased when he suggested he walk her home.

The sun was just setting when they headed towards her house. She was quiet beside him and kept her eyes on the path ahead. A little nervous about what to say to him, she chose to walk in silence.

Aaron walked beside her. He had gotten the impression from Todd and Megan that she was usually in charge of, well, everything. It was nice to see her jump, when he had brushed up against her as he reached for a dish.

As they walked, he could hear crickets chirping and frogs calling out to find a mate. At one point, he even heard an owl hooting, and then all was silent. He took in a deep breath of fresh air and enjoyed the smells of pine. This is what he had wanted, no, what he needed.

When they reached the fork in the path, she turned to face him. "You don't have to walk me all the way. I can make it home myself."

"What? You might be grabbed on the way back to your house? No, I'll make sure you get to your door safe and sound," he said, smiling down at her.

"The only one that's been grabbing me is you," she said, turning her back on him and starting to march away.

He grabbed her shoulders and turned her back to face him. Looking down into her face, he could see the fear and the hurt he had caused.

"I'll apologize for that. There was no excuse for my actions." He shook his head, still holding her firm. He could remember feeling hurt not too long ago. Releasing her shoulders, he turned and started walking back down the path.

"It was nice meeting you, Lacey. Have a good night," he said over his shoulder as he continued toward his house.

"Good night," she said under her breath. She stared at his back, then turned down her own path. She thought about the day's events and the man she'd just met. She wondered what she'd gotten herself into.

CHAPTER 3

*L*acey loved Saturday nights. She usually didn't work the floor but had stepped in to help when they were busy. She had sweat rolling between her shoulder blades, a juice stain on her shirt, and she was sure there was a small blister on her right heel. But she had a smile on her face.

Saturdays were always busy at the Golden Oar, her family's restaurant, and Lacey loved them. This was when families came in for a night out away from their kitchens, and couples came in for dates and dimly lit tables.

She adored this small town and the fact that she knew everyone by name, and she liked almost every last person. She was serving the Bergman's, a family of nine in the dining hall, when she felt a shiver run up her spine. Setting a plate down, she turned her head slightly to the left and spotted the cause of her disturbance.

He stood in the doorway, and the young hostess, Katie, was trying to get his attention so she could seat him.

He wore an old pair of jeans with a small hole in one knee, old tennis shoes, and a UCLA t-shirt that had seen better days. His hair was messed up like he had run his hands through it, and he had a smudge of dirt on his chin. He looked great. He gave her one of his big smiles, and Katie proceeded to lead him to one of the tables in her section.

After clearing her drink tray, she headed over to Aaron's table. She'd hoped that after the other night, she wouldn't see him for a while. She really wished she would stop thinking of him.

"Hi, can I get you something to drink?" she asked, while handing him a menu.

"Hi," he said, as he smiled up at her.

"Hi," she said back, when he continued to look at her, she piped in. "We've a lovely Merlot, or perhaps you prefer a Chardonnay?" She could feel her frustration building as he continued to smile at her as she proceeded to run through the whole drink menu.

"You look very appealing in that outfit." He continued to smile at her without once looking down at his menu.

In her building frustration, she forgot to hide her astonishment, and her mouth dropped open.

When he had walked into the crowded restaurant, he expected something different from the very comfortable environment full of happy patrons. The place felt like home. It was hard to explain, but it felt … right.

He had just finished a quick scan of the restaurant with its nautical theme when he spotted Lacey serving food to a big family in the back corner. The first thing he noticed was the outfit. He appreciated the short black skirt that showed off her legs; she looked very appealing.

He enjoyed watching the way she moved through the room and tables like she was on a mission. Then he was treated to her rehearsed citation of the restaurant's drink menu. He felt, that listening to that sexy voice was never going to be a hardship. However, he thought it was his duty to throw her off balance, and gauging by her expression, he was sure he had succeeded.

"I'll have a beer, please," he said when she closed her mouth. He could see her eyes starting to fire up with frustration.

She turned on her heels and marched off without a word. He smiled and enjoyed watching her walk away.

Less than a minute later, a tall man came out the kitchen doors, scanned the room, and marched towards his table with determination.

The man was easily a half foot taller than him, but their builds were similar.

"Can I help you?" asked the man as he came to a stop in front of Aaron's table. Aaron thought he heard a hint of an accent but couldn't quite put his finger on it.

"Yes, I believe I'm ready to order," he said, looking down at his menu. When he received no response, he looked back up at the man. He had a confused expression on his face and then it dawned on Aaron. The man had the same silver eyes as Lacey, the same black hair, and even the same dip in the chin. This must be Lacey's brother, Iian, who was deaf. Setting the menu down, Aaron signed his greeting.

"Hello, you must be Iian. I'm Dr. Aaron Stevens. Todd has told me so much about you and this restaurant. I thought I'd come and check it out for myself."

"Dr. Stevens? You're Dr. Steven's grandson?" Iian signed back, looking surprised and relieved. When Lacey had come back to the kitchen complaining about the "jerk" at table eleven, he had marched out to take care of the man.

"Yes, yes, I am."

Iian smiled back at him. "May I join you for a few minutes?" When Aaron nodded, Iian sat in one of the empty chairs.

"It's good to finally meet the man who took such good

care of Megan. I heard you're taking over your grandfather's practice."

The conversation was light and friendly; Aaron figured he would like Iian as much as he liked Todd. Both brothers were friendly and very protective of their loved ones.

Iian and Aaron were laughing when Lacey came back over with Aaron's beer.

She had been surprised to see the doctor using sign to talk to Iian and could not help but notice his hands moving fluently with the language. She felt her heart rate increase as she stared at them. They were large and tan, and she tried not to imagine what they would feel like all over her body. Both men looked up at her and smiled, and she quickly pulled her eyes back to Aaron's face.

"Well, Doctor, have you decided what you want?" She pulled out her pad and pencil.

When she was met with silence, she peered over at him. He was giving her a funny look with another one of his goofy smiles.

For the second time that night, she felt her cheeks heat and quickly looked over at Iian who was smiling back at her.

"I'm still working on it," he said with a smile.

Iian had never seen Lacey this way before; her face was flushed, and he was sure she was blushing. Iian had the feeling that he had been completely forgotten.

"What time do you get off work?" Aaron asked. Just then, Iian stood up, laughed loudly, and walked back to the kitchen shaking his head.

"Let's get this out in the open," she said, pointing her pen in his direction. "I don't like pushy men. I don't know where you come from, but around here..." she trailed off when she noticed he wasn't paying attention to her anymore. His eyes were on her face, but she could see that they had filled with sadness. She took a deep breath and sat down across from him, placing her hand on his.

"Where did you just go?" she whispered.

He looked across the table at her. Her eyes showed concern instead of the resentment he had seen a second earlier. He shook his head to clear it. Of course, he had been thinking of his ex-girlfriend Jennifer. He'd tried to completely wipe her from his mind, but she kept sneaking back in.

Looking across the table at Lacey, who was the complete opposite of Jennifer, he wondered why he was so fascinated by her. She was unlike any woman he had ever been interested in before.

He liked tall, blonde, athletic types. So why did he have an urge, one that came from deep down inside, to get to know Lacey? Was he willing to chance a relationship again? Could he afford the cost again, if things went wrong?

Lacey saw his eyes focusing slowly on her and then glanced down to their joined hands. She pulled her hand away quickly.

"She did a number on you," she whispered.

"Who?" he said, shrugging, while trying to act casual.

Lacey shook her head. "Listen, Doctor…" she began.

"Can you call me Aaron? When you call me Doctor it almost sounds like an insult." He smiled over at her and pulled her hand back into his. Lacey tugged on her hand after she saw his eyes were focused and full of mischief.

"Did you come here to eat dinner? Doctor?" she said as she stood and grasped her note pad and pen tightly.

He laughed and placed his order. As she marched back towards the kitchen, he wondered what it would take to get inside that little bundle of energy.

By closing time, Lacey's feet were burning. As she helped

clean up the dining area, she realized she enjoyed Saturday nights, but she also welcomed Sunday mornings.

The Doctor had left after filling himself with a full plate of appetizers, a huge steak and shrimp dinner, and a plate of apple pie a la mode.

She had two brothers, so she knew what it took to feed a man. However, she guessed that neither Todd or Iian would've packed away as much food as Aaron just had.

She knew he was remodeling the old Bell place, so she thought that maybe he hadn't eaten since the dinner at Todd's the other night. He had downed almost as much food then, too.

If there was one thing Lacey prided herself on, it was seeing to the people of Pride. And now, however uncomfortable he made her, he was one of those people.

She could not understand the discomfort she felt; after all, he had been a perfect gentleman the rest of the evening, and he had left her a large enough tip.

It wouldn't hurt to visit the old Bell place tomorrow; she knew his offices were closed on the weekends. Maybe she would just stop by after church. After all, she mused, it would be the Christian thing to do.

She was curious to see what he was doing to the house. She also wondered about the hurt look in his eyes, and about the woman who had put it there.

CHAPTER 4

*A*ttending Church always made Lacey feel more level. She found Father Michael's voice soothing and often blocked out his words, letting the feeling and mood of the service seep into her instead. He was a priest who believed in preaching at the congregation instead of to them. She enjoyed the energy he brought; it gave her the extra push she needed to start the week. Todd and Megan had come to several services after their wedding, but this weekend they were missing. Lacey knew Megan wasn't Catholic, but she could tell Megan enjoyed being a part of the small community.

Iian had not been to church in some time; Lacey remembered it was right after the accident when he stopped attending.

After the service, Lacey found herself cornered by the usual group of elderly women. Lacey dubbed them the *"Hens of Pride"*, but never said this to their faces. She had grown up with these women being a part of her life and could handle their gossiping natures for the most part. However, today they seemed more organized and seemed to have a purpose.

"Of course, you've heard about the new doctor, he's such a fine young man," Betty, one of the shortest in the group, piped up. She had lost her husband recently to cancer, which, to Lacey's thinking, gave the woman an edge in the group.

"I had an appointment with him last week. You know my gout has been acting up, again. Well, I can tell you, he is such an attractive young thing. Remolded the whole office too; the place looks brand new. Have you been by to see him yet, Lacey? He would be about your age and such a nice looking fellow…."

At this point the entire group turned their eyes to her. She knew that look; matchmakers all of them.

Smiling she replied, "Yes, the doctor and I have met on several occasions. We've even shared a few dinners together."

With this news, Lacey turned and walked away, leaving the ladies with a fresh wave of gossip to release into the town. Lacey felt her work had been done for the day. Smiling even larger, she walked over to where Dr. Stevens Sr. stood.

To say the man was old was an understatement. He was about her height, had thin silver hair, and the apparently the heart of a man half his age. She remembered a time when she was little, she thought of him as the biggest man in town.

"How are you this morning, Dr. Stevens?" Lacey took his outstretched hand. It looked frail, but his grip was still firm.

"Oh, I'm fine. I'm enjoying the weather and have been out fishing almost every day." He shook his head and leaned closer to Lacey. "Bored out of my mind. I'm not sure what to do with myself most days."

Shaking her head, she smiled. "Well, you know there are a few good-looking women standing over there who would love to help you occupy some of that free time." She figured turnabout was fair play.

Lacey glanced back to the group of women she had

just left. All of them were facing her and talking amongst themselves. When they noticed Dr. Steven's head turning their way, they all looked away quickly. All, that is, except Betty, who fluffed her hair and wet her lips. Lacey was trying to tease the old man, but she could see now there were sparks flying between the pair. Smiling even more, she patted his arm.

He cleared his throat. "Yes, well, have you met my grandson, yet? Strapping young lad. I'm very proud he decided to follow my profession. It's a pity his folks didn't take more interest in him. I'm afraid I didn't raise my own son very well," he said, shaking his head.

"I've had the pleasure of meeting Aaron on several occasions. It seems to me your son did a fine job raising him." She patted his hand.

"Boarding schools!" Dr. Stevens said, shaking his head again.

"I beg your pardon?"

"The boy was raised in boarding schools. Only came out to visit me for a few weeks every other summer; never really did get a lot of time with his folks. They were too busy jetting around the world. That poor boy never really knew what it was like to be part of a true family." Lacey felt something shift inside her. She tried to stamp it down, so the guilt would not outweigh her feelings.

"I've been asking that boy to come to Pride for years. I guess the timing was never right for him before. But he is here now; maybe he will settle down and start his own family. Your Pa knew how to raise a family; strong morals, healthy bodies, lots of love. Now there's a family setting my poor Aaron needed," he finished off, looking over her shoulder.

Lacey looked over and saw Betty walking towards them. "Well, I better get going," she said quickly. She was sure the doctor hadn't heard her last words because he was frantically trying to straighten his blazer.

After leaving the good doctor, she was stopped several times by other people on the way to her car. She enjoyed catching up with everyone in her town.

By the time Lacey left the church parking lot, she had a slight headache that was starting to go full throttle. But she was committed to being neighborly and bringing the new doctor lunch, so she pointed her car in the direction of the old Bell place. The road to the house was poorly maintained. She knew the house had needed a lot of work, but nothing prepared her for what she saw when she arrived at the end of the drive.

The yard was a jungle of overgrown trees and bushes that covered one third of the house. She could see the house was in dire need of sanding and a good paint job, maybe a new roof to boot.

The covered porch was falling down and would have to be replaced entirely. Off to the left by the garage, there was a new pile of building materials covered with a blue tarp, no doubt materials to do just that.

The garage doors were open, and she could see Aaron working with a table saw, cutting a long piece of wood in half.

He wore protective glasses and ear plugs. Lacey smiled at the tool belt that was strapped around his narrow waist it was pulling his pants slightly down with the added weight.

When she stepped from the car and shut the door, he made no move, and she knew he hadn't seen or heard her drive up.

She walked over and watched his back as she leaned against the door frame and enjoyed the view. What a back! He sure was tall and broad, his arms wide and his waist narrow. Her eyes wandered down, and she enjoyed the way his jeans fit his butt. She remembered what he had looked like at the pond and realized he looked even better in faded blue jeans. She knew that she was blushing; her cheeks felt like they were on fire.

Pulling her eyes back up to his shoulders, she looked at his hair. It was golden, curly, looked like it would be very soft to the touch, and was a little longer than her own. She imagined running her fingers through it and felt a little jealous of the curl he had. Her hair was straight. At one point she had tried to grow it out, but she didn't have the patience for it. She had chopped it off and kept it short ever since.

When he finished cutting the wood and flicked off the saw, she said. "Hi."

He jumped while spinning around, dropping the piece of wood directly on his ankle.

"Son of a --" he cursed, jumping up and down on his other foot.

Lacey quickly walked over and grabbed his hand, then led him to a stool a few feet away.

"Here, let me look at it." She bent over and pulled his pant leg up, so she could view his hurt ankle.

AARON HAD BEEN SHOCKED when he heard her sexy voice, because he'd been trying to get her out of his mind all morning. He figured he could work off his interest in her and was trying really hard. But then, here she was in the flesh, rubbing her small hands all over his ankle. He could smell her, scent and the pain in his ankle disappeared. Her dark head was bent over his leg as she pulled down his sock.

"Trying to get me naked again?" he said with a laugh when her fingers tickled his skin.

She jerked her hand back and glared up at him. Taking a

deep breath, she stood up and made a show of straightening her dark pink skirt.

"Must you be so crude when I came out here to bring you some lunch?   But it appears you're busy and in no mood to eat…" she trailed off when he abruptly stood and grabbed her shoulders lightly.

"You brought me lunch?" he asked, his face was lit with amusement. Jennifer had never cooked. Her idea of making food was calling the local Chinese takeout.

"I'm sorry, I'll try to behave," he said eagerly.

She gave him a look that said she doubted he would ever behave. Then she walked over to her car and picked up the basket, which he immediately took from her.

"Please, come in," He motioned for her to walk to the front door and followed her into the house.

She had only taken two steps into the door when she stopped. "You can't be living here?" she gasped as she looked around.

There were no inside walls; the place was totally gutted. There was no carpet, no walls, and the ceiling was gone. She could see the exposed trusses that held the roof in place. All that remained were the outside walls, lots of wires, and various pipes hanging in midair.

She saw a sleeping bag in one corner with a box next to it with an alarm clock, phone, and a lamp sitting on top.

There was an old green toilet in one corner with a shower stall next to a small green sink. There were no walls or doors that separated the space for privacy. There was no kitchen, no refrigerator or stove, nothing but a big empty space.

She'd been in the house years ago and remembered the kitchen should have been off the back, but now, all that remained was emptiness.

"It's not that bad. Although I've been thinking about

finishing the kitchen, first." He smiled when his stomach growled.

There was a wooden box and a chair next to the sleeping bag. Aaron walked towards them carrying the basket and placed it on top of a cooler.

Lacey had yet to say anything else; she was still in shock. She finally walked over and sat on the only chair, watching as he set the food out on the table.

"Why are you here?" she asked, watching his eyes flash with surprise.

"I was going to ask you the same question."

"When you were at the restaurant last night, I realized you might not have a working kitchen," she said, looking around. "Now I realize you don't have a working anything."

"I'm making progress," he said, shoving half a piece of chicken in his mouth. After swallowing, he continued, "It's like camping. Besides, it's coming along faster than I had imagined."

"You call this," she gestured to the empty house, "coming along?"

"Sure." He bent over and scooped up some potatoes. "You should have seen it yesterday." He looked over giving her a lopsided smile.

"Why?" On his blank look, she repeated her question, "Why are you here?"

"My grandfather asked me to take over his practice. Besides," he shrugged his shoulders, "it's about time he retired, and I thought it was a good idea at the time."

"And now?" she asked. He smiled over at her.

"I talked to your grandfather this morning at church," she continued. "He says he's been asking you to come to Pride for years. Why now?" She leaned over and took a roll and began to nibble on it.

"Is this your way of telling me you're interested?" he leaned closer.

She made sure to shut her mouth this time and took a breath before saying very clearly, "No!" She tried not to blush.

He laughed. "You're awful easy to rile up," he said, smiling over at her. "You're very pretty when you blush." He laughed again, then went back to eating.

She went from embarrassment to anger so fast, he could have sworn he saw smoke coming off her skin. Standing up and setting the roll down, she turned and looked down at him.

He looked like a six-year-old at a picnic. He was sitting there on a wooden box with a small paper plate packed full of food balanced on his knees, his mouth full of potatoes. She would have found it funny, if she weren't so anger.

"Is this some kind of joke to you? Let's see what it takes to get Lacey all riled up? Is that it? Well, let me tell you something, buster …" she said, pointing at him.

"You come into my town, *my town!* And you jump into my pond, *my pond!* And you grope me, getting me all mixed up. You look at me like you want to…to…" she broke off, and then tossing her hands around, and began to pace in front of him.

"Now you sit over there eating my food – m*y food!* – telling me that you like to see me angry. Well you can forget it. Your games are not going to work on me. Let's get something straight here, Doctor Stevens." She bent over him and shoved her finger into his chest.

"You can take your games and shove them. I don't play games and I certainly don't want to play with you."

She straightened back up and turned to walk out. She made it halfway across the empty room before she was spun around and found her mouth being crushed to his.

He had sat through her speech, enjoying her beauty and her sexy voice; when she was mad she was exquisite. When she had stormed towards the door, he had to catch her; and his body had acted before his brain had jumped into gear.

He knew he was being rough with her and could feel her soft lips under his. His hands were on her back, holding her close to him as she struggled against his chest, arousing him even more.

He pulled his head back and looked into her eyes. "I lose all self-control when I'm around you."

"You jerk! Let me go!" she struggled against his chest lightly.

She could see his eyes were unfocused; he had a lost expression on his face. Her hands were crushed between their bodies, her fingers flat on his chest. She could feel his heart racing under them and if she wanted to, could count the beats. Her heart was racing, matching his.

He pulled back a little but didn't release her. He shook his head, and she could see his eyes clearing.

"Damn you," she whispered. Pulling one hand free, she yanked his head back down to hers and went up on her toes to meet his lips once more.

His lips were soft this time as she rubbed hers gently over his. When she deepened the kiss, she felt his hands slide down her back to her hips as he pulled her closer.

She tasted so good he had to hold back a moan. When he ran his hands up and down her small spine, he felt her shiver and felt his own body spasm in response.

She was small, but a nice armful. He pulled her body higher, so their chests met and her feet were off the ground completely, his mouth never leaving hers. He started walking backwards to where his air mattress and sleeping bag sat on the floor.

When he reached it, he pulled her down with him, shifting her under him. She stiffened and pulled away; then pushed on his chest until he released her.

"No." She stood up, straightening her clothes as she backed away. The fear he saw in her eyes allowed him to let her go. "I'm not ready."

"What's your game, Lacey?" he whispered to her back as he watched her race across the floor and out his front door.

CHAPTER 5

Over the next few weeks Aaron was busy with work at the office and construction on his house. He was working his ass off, and he hurt in places he shouldn't. The cold nights had forced him to move his sleeping bag right in front of the fireplace in the living room. The heating and air conditioning unit he had purchased would be installed after the air ducts were in place, but for now he was enjoying the fireplace.

He'd done all the plumbing himself. It had been an easy enough task, and he had even installed his new tankless water heater, making showers more enjoyable. Laying all the raw electric wires in all the walls had been easy enough as well, and he couldn't wait until he had lights other than the construction lights that ran off the generator.

The window company had come and gone in two days, installing every window, and also the front door. He enjoyed the new glass sliding doors off the dining room and the master bedroom.

He was really enjoying seeing the place come together. It had been years, since he had worked this hard on something that he had wanted so badly. All his life, he had wanted to live in a "*home*". High rise apartments and high-end hotels had filled his young life until boarding schools had taken over and his parents had pretty much disappeared from his life. Turning back to the task at hand, he noticed all the work that was still needed.

Drywall was going to be a bitch. It was taking all his strength and patience to hang every piece. He had just finished hanging his third piece, which had taken him almost an hour, when he heard a car drive up.

Looking out his new front bay windows, he saw Todd's Jeep. He switched off the generator and pulled down his dust mask. This was a good time to take a break. He walked over and opened the front door just as Todd went to ring the doorbell.

"It doesn't work yet," Aaron said, leaning back against the door. "Matter of fact, nothing electric works yet." Smiling, they shook hands.

"Come on in," Aaron said, stepping back.

Todd stepped into a room that had a pile of drywall sitting in the middle of the floor.

"You sure have done a lot of work. Lacey mentioned what you were doing over here. I thought I would see if you needed a hand."

Then he looked at Aaron's clothes, which were covered with fine white drywall powder.

"You aren't trying to hang drywall by yourself, are you?" Todd asked.

"I thought it would be easy, like hanging wallpaper. The bitch weighs a ton and cracks and breaks if you don't support it just right." Aaron threw up his hands in frustration.

Shaking his head, Todd pulled out his cell phone and

started to text someone, saying, "We'll see what we can do about that."

Half an hour later, Iian walked in the door with two other men. They all had their own tools. Iian carried a container of sandwiches, and another man had a case of beer.

As the men got to work, Aaron admitted it helped to have more arms and backs helping. It only took three hours to finish hanging the living room and kitchen drywall.

Everyone left well after dark with a promise to be back first thing Saturday morning to help finish the rest of the place.

It felt weird to have neighbors who actually helped and cared. It didn't hurt to have them bring over loads of food and beer every time they helped either.

The men had returned as promised and in three days the drywall was completed. Walls made the place feel a little more closed in, but the rooms were still huge and airy.

IT HAD BEEN a few weeks since she'd last been over to Aaron's place. She had seen him once at the market, but she'd quickly ducked into the back room and waited him out. She knew it was small of her. She couldn't believe she'd hidden from him like that, but she couldn't help it; she needed more time to think about everything. She tried to keep herself busy at the restaurant to keep him off her mind. There were always things to do – new night staff to train, financial books to work on. But after spending days looking for a lost eighteen dollars in the books only to realize that she had just read two numbers backwards, she realized it wasn't working. How could a man affect her so much that she couldn't even see numbers right? She had to face it. She couldn't get the man out of her mind. To be honest, she didn't know if she even wanted him out.

Then, to top the week off, she had been cornered in the grocery store last night by several of the younger church women. She hadn't even seen it coming. How could she have not seen it coming?

THERE WAS A STORM BREWING OUTSIDE, one that almost matched Aaron's mood.

He'd had enough of Lacey's cat and mouse game, it was time he went on the hunt. He grabbed his coat and his keys and left the house, determined to end the game tonight.

He'd seen her ducking in the back room of the market a few days ago. He'd even seen her quick exit from the restaurant the other night. It appeared she was avoiding him, but that would stop tonight. He would go to her place and if she wasn't there, he would go down to the restaurant and find her. She was bound to be somewhere; he was determined to see her tonight.

He'd never seen the Jordan's house, but knew their place was at the end of the road. After a few minutes of bumping down the dirt road, he came to the clearing where the house sat. It was bigger than he'd imagined. He'd seen manors like this in England when he had traveled the countryside during his college years and he could just imagine the stone two-story manor stood there waiting for him to slay the dragon, so he could cart off the fair Lacey from her room in the high tower.

He saw lights coming from the windows and turning into the circular drive as he saw a shadow cross one of the windows near the front door. Pulling up behind Lacey's car, he turned off the engine and dashed through the rain towards the house.

LACEY ALWAYS LOVED the weeks before Halloween, the best season for movies. For weeks before the scary night, she would hang around the house and watch, her favorite horror movies.

Zombies, vampires, and werewolves were on almost every channel and she tried to watch them all. She'd watch while bathing, dressing, and eating, but especially loved watching them while cooking, like she was doing now.

She had the small flat screen on the far kitchen wall playing the old black-and-white classic Dracula. She loved the music, the lack of color, the overly dramatic actors, and the suspense.

Iian was working the late shift tonight, leaving her alone in the big house, which only made the scary movies better. She'd already watched two other classics when the urge to cook had called her to the kitchen. The cooking urge was something Lacey knew never to ignore.

Feeling inspired, she cranked up the sound on the TV and went to town, putting together spicy turkey meatloaf, baby potatoes with onions, and a side of green peppers. She was chopping up a tomato and carrots for the salad when she heard a sound, which caused her to jump while screaming louder than the heroine in the movie.

STANDING on the covered front porch, Aaron was about to knock when Bernard raced up to him, shook off the rain, then sat at his feet. After a few pets and a quick belly rub, the dog walked off towards the side of the house. He stopped and looked over his shoulder at Aaron, as if to say, "this way."

Following the dog's lead, Aaron took the small stone path around to the side of the house, where he could see the lights on in the kitchen. The windows were big, and the curtains were opened wide, so he could see the entire kitchen and the TV set.

He could see Lacey by the counter. She was wearing a bright green and yellow sweater that hung low over her shoulders, with a pair of dark gray leggings underneath. Her socks had glowing green ghosts with bright yellow eyes.

He could also see that she was totally immersed in an old, Dracula movie. She stood leaning on the counter, her eyes glued to the set. He knocked loudly on the door.

It took Lacey several heartbeats to recover from the shock of seeing Aaron through the back-glass door. She walked over and yanked it open.

"Good evening," he said, in a voice that mimicked the blood sucker on her television set.

"What the hell do you think you're doing? You scared the hell out of me!" she said, smacking him on the shoulder. Bernard sneaked in the open door between the pair.

He reached up and rubbed his shoulder, pretending to be hurt. "Is this how you greet your visitors?"

She glared back at him.

"Oh, come on, Lacey, I've missed seeing you around. You've been keeping yourself scarce." He lifted his eyebrows and smiled.

When she didn't respond, he piped in, "Aren't you going to invite me in?" His Transylvania accent was terrible, and she continued to glare.

"You don't know how long it's been since I've had a good meal, and whatever you're cooking smells so good. Plus, remember, over there in that empty house, I have no furniture, no kitchen, no TV…" he dropped the smile and tried for a pathetic puppy look. If it worked for Bernard, who was now comfortably curled up on a dog bed in the corner, it might just work for him.

Remembering his empty house, she caved. She may have been avoiding him for the last couple weeks, but that didn't mean she hadn't worried about the fact that he was still living in an unfinished house. She stepped back so he could walk in but instead, he pulled her into his arm for a kiss that was soft and sweet. She could taste him, he smelled like spring rain.

"If you don't let go of me, my potatoes are going to burn." He released her, and she rushed over to the stove. "You might as well come in and stay; I've made enough."

"Thanks," he said, removing his wet jacket. She saw he wore a light gray t-shirt that stretched across his shoulders. He quickly walked over to her and kissed her again. This kiss was fast and potent.

"That's what I've been missing." At her frustrated look, he walked past her and sat at the table.

As she checked on her potatoes, she wondered how he could look so good in an old pair of faded jeans and a t-shirt.

They ate in the living room, sitting at the coffee table, so they could watch an old werewolf movie.

After eating, Aaron tried to pay attention to the movie, he really did, but she smelled intoxicating. It was something flowery and soft. She sat next to him on the sofa with her legs tucked up and her eyes focused on the screen. He would steal looks at her from the corner of his eyes and as far as he could tell, she was engrossed in film. He noticed she didn't even flinch at the scary parts.

How was he supposed to pay attention to an old black-and-white film when her profile looked so interesting?

Her hair hung over her forehead, and her small nose had

a little upturn at the tip. Her cheeks, he remembered, were soft. Her lips had the look of a cute pout. He was thinking of the dip in the middle of her chin when he realized he could look at her all night.

As smoothly as he could, he swung his arm over the back of the couch and moved closer until he had pulled her into the crook of his arm. He felt her tense a little, but then she released her breath and settled in. He smiled to himself and pulled her closer. Leaning his head down, he started playing his tongue across her earlobe. He heard her breath catch, heard her moan, and then he lost control.

Lacey felt his hot breath on her neck and closed her eyes, not realizing she had let out a small moan. The next thing she knew he was kissing her, making her forget the movie. His hands slowly and lightly roamed over her body, creating little goose bumps wherever they touched. She felt like she was floating, then she realized he had repositioned them, so his back was now flat on the couch. He was pulling her on top of him.

Her arms reached around and pulled him closer as he devoured her mouth. He tasted of dinner and wine, and somehow the mixture was intoxicating. Running her hands over his shoulders she thought she felt him shiver. Was he affected by their kisses as she was? She started to explore his arms and then moved her hands around to his back.

He felt lost. He was sure his whole body was shaking while her hands roamed over his torso. Holding himself in check, he reached behind her and pulled her closer. He started to run his hands slowly under her sweater and then freed her undershirt. When he reached underneath to her skin, he heard her breath catch, and when his fingers explored the soft skin on her lower back, she released another low moan and pushed herself closer. She was so small and soft; he realized he had to have more.

Covering her with his mouth, his hands roamed lower and lower…

Just then the dog let out a quick bark and darted towards the front door. They both heard a car drive up, and Lacey quickly sat up and proceeded to fix her sweater. Aaron sat up as Iian walked in the front door.

IIAN WAS IN A FOUL MOOD. Not only had the new chef not worked out tonight, but two of his kitchen staff had the flu, which left him three hands short in the kitchen. He hated interviewing new chefs. Not only was the process hard, due to his lack of hearing, but he was sure he had exhausted the pool of talented chefs, both in Pride and in the neighboring towns.

When he noticed Aaron's car in front of house, he smiled for the first time that day. Giving his sister grief about Aaron was something to look forward to at least. It had been months since Iian had dated and he only thought it fair that Lacey enjoy some of his frustration when it came to relationships. His sister, who had always seemed in control of every aspect of her life, seemed nothing but frustrated and dazed around the doctor.

Smiling a little, he opened the door just as the pair jumped apart on the couch. This made him smile even more. What a great ending to a terrible day; this was going to be fun.

CHAPTER 6

*O*ver the next few days it seemed everywhere Lacey went, Aaron was there.

When she was at the grocery market getting some cinnamon for her homemade rolls, he had magically materialized behind her. He had continued to walk around the small store with her as she collected her items, frustrating her. Her cheeks had heated to a toasty red by the time they reached the checkout. She had been so flustered, she had forgotten half of the items on her list.

Now, as she stood in her kitchen and added more flour to her cinnamon rolls, she thought of how the whole town was probably talking about her and Aaron. She remembered how Mary, from church had discreetly followed the pair around the store, at a safe distance, of course, listening to them.

Aaron didn't help matters. It seemed he was always touching her; either her elbow while they were walking, or holding her hand, or even touching the back of her neck below her hair line. Remembering this, she stopped stirring her dough and reached up with a flour covered hand to feel the spot on her neck.

Taking a deep breath now, she continued to stir the dough mixture with more vigor.

She had spent years building up a spitfire reputation around town. She was sure this was going to hurt it.

Dumping the dough out of the bowl, she started to knead it and thought about how Aaron had helped her take her groceries out to her car and kissed her. Kissed her! Right in front of the store windows. In front of everyone!

Lacey swore she heard a hush fall over the town in that moment, and was sure that the moments following were filled with a buzz that flew outwards as the event was retold to everyone within a hundred-mile radius.

Feeling her cheeks burn, she looked down and realized she was holding the dough in her hands as if her small fingers were wrapped around Aaron's neck. Plopping it back on the counter, she proceeded to beat the heck out of it.

Her rolls were probably going to be tough and dry thanks to Dr. Stevens.

Before he'd come into town, she had prided herself on her reputation. She was sure that was the reason most people kept clear of her and her personal life. But now, after a kiss outside the market, she might as well be wearing a sign on her chest that read, "*Give me any and all advice on dating.*" Just earlier that day, someone had attempted to give her advice on how to maintain a good relationship.

Relationship? Dating? Was that what they were doing?

She paused as she placed the dough in a big bowl.

Just because she felt funny when she saw Aaron, did not mean she wanted a relationship with him? Did it?

She shrugged and set a cloth on top of the bowl and set it aside to let it rise. Starting her clean-up process before she started making her famous cinnamon and sugar glaze, she tried to relax. Baking always made her feel more centered.

How could a doctor, let alone a very attractive man, be after her? She always tried to keep her head down and had learned in the past to stay clear of "beautiful" men. What little experience she had in the past with the opposite sex, never seemed to turn out for the best. It wasn't that she was scared of men, but she had learned early in life to be wary of men with promises and big smiles. Aaron's smile was one of the biggest and brightest she'd ever seen.

She was halfway through cleaning when she realized she was using window cleaner on the counter where she had mixed her dough. Looking down, she saw the big blue glob of cleaner and dry flour. She couldn't even clean properly without Aaron getting in the way. Throwing her rag down in frustration, she started cleaning up the mess correctly.

What was a man like that doing here? More importantly, what would it take to keep a man like that interested in staying in Pride?

What the hell was he doing here?

Looking across the empty space that was soon to be his kitchen, he came up blank. He could close his eyes and see what it was he wanted, yet when he opened them, nothing seemed right.

The place still looked empty, but thanks to the Jordan brothers, he now had drywall. He'd even hired a few local guys to do the tape and texture on the walls. They should be finishing up tomorrow, which meant he had to figure out the layout of his kitchen tonight.

He remembered reading somewhere about the kitchen triangle rule, but for the life of him couldn't remember what it was. He had done the wiring and plumbing in the kitchen in such a way that he would have options.

Looking across the space, he still came up blank. Should he put the refrigerator there or across the room? He knew the sink could go over there under the window, but he thought it might go just as nicely on the island facing his living room.

Then there was the stove. He had the electric in place and knew exactly where it belonged, or so he thought.

Was it against some kitchen rule to have the stove too close to your refrigerator?

Taking a big breath, he stepped back, closed his eyes, and tried to picture himself standing in the room making a simple meal. He opened his eyes when nothing came to mind.

"Fine then, let's try something else." He closed his eyes once more.

This time out of the darkness he saw Lacey's face; she was smiling. Good. Then he pictured her shoulders and arms as they were busy with a simple task of chopping fresh vegetables on a wood cutting board...his cutting board.

She stood chopping them on the island in the center of the kitchen...his kitchen.

The sink was in place under the window and the gas stove top sat on the island next to her, with a pan sizzling with some type of meat. He could almost smell the rich food she was making.

A glass door refrigerator sat on the opposite wall, stocked with fresh items. A pair of double stacked ovens sat across the room.

Then Lacey turned and put the vegetables into the pan while she smiled at him.

He almost lost his concentration, but he refocused on the walls and cabinets. He could see they were dark color, maybe dark oak -- no -- cherry cabinets with glass doors on a few cupboards here and there. The walls were a nice rich olive green. Four bar stools sat on the bar side of the island.

Opening his eyes, he got to work making her kitchen.

IT WAS on one of Lacey's many runs to take food over to Megan's bed and breakfast that it happened. She was arranging the turkey sandwiches, fresh baked rolls, and homemade macadamia nut cookies when Megan squealed.

"What? What's wrong?" Lacey rushed to Megan's side. Then she noticed that Megan had a smile on her face and she was laughing. Lacey, pale and shaking, finally figured it out.

"Did the baby just kick? Oh, let me feel." She placed her hands-on Megan's round belly.

Megan smiled and covered Lacey's hands with her own just as the baby kicked again.

Just then, Todd walked in to see his sister kneeling on the floor in front of his wife. He noticed they had identical smiles and both had a hand on Megan's belly.

"What, what's wrong?" He rushed over to his wife.

"Your son or daughter was showing us how excited he or she is that Auntie Lacey was here."

Lacey stood up and stepped back, enjoying the scene. Her brother was kissing his wife and their hands were now joined over the movement of the new life they had created.

To have a second chance is an incredible gift, but for these two people to have that chance was something indescribable.

Leaving the pair to enjoy the moment, she quietly went out to the dining area and finished setting up the food for the guests. Lately, it seemed, there had been a lot of guests coming and going at the B&B. So many guests, that she and Iian had been busy stocking the place with meals.

Todd had been helping out. Lately, he had been taking more and more time off from running the shipping company. He was working from his home office all the time now. She was sure it was due to his fear for Megan and the baby's health. But, both mom and baby were very healthy and progressing nicely. Lacey could tell Megan was not only feeling well, but that pregnancy suited her.

THAT NIGHT, Lacey and Bernard took a walk on the beach. Her mind was preoccupied with Aaron, and she hoped the crisp evening air would help her settle and organize those thoughts. She enjoyed the seclusion, that the strip of beach below her house provided.

Bernard had a piece of driftwood in his mouth. It was longer than he was, but he dragged it along the beach, leaving a jagged line in the wet sand. His tail never stopped wagging, and it was clear that he was hoping to play chase with the giant stick. Leaning over, she picked up a smaller chunk of wood and tossed it into the surf. Dropping the larger piece, he chased after it as it was being tossed around in the waves.

Lacey could tell that storms would soon bring the cold waters up closer to the shore to pound against the dark rocks, that lined her beach.

If she closed her eyes, she could remember her mother, here on a warm sunny day building a sand castle. Her mother was heavily pregnant with Iian. She had been so young, younger actually than Lacey was right now.

Walking in the wet soft sand, Lacey shook her bangs out of her eyes and thought about getting another hair cut.

Bending over to pick up the chunk of wood and giving it another toss for Bernard, she started thinking about the doctor. She was seeing a lot of him now and not just around town.

She bent down to throw Bernard the stick again, flinging it out to the left along the shore, as she thought about her past dating experiences.

It's not as if she hadn't dated at all; she hadn't been looking for men to date recently. Every man in town knew her and her family. Most men her age were already settled into families themselves. And the one's that weren't, well, she wasn't interested. Growing up with protective brothers had kept most of the town boys away, but she had managed to go on some dates.

As she threw Bernard's stick again, she thought about her life choices. Traveling a bit after school had been an enjoyment for her. Traveling and never staying in one place long enough to get close to anyone had been what she'd wanted. She had returned home only to have to deal with the family crisis shortly after. Her father had died and that had consumed her life for several years. Dating was one of the last things on her mind at the time.

When Aaron's face came into mind, she sat down on an old log and took a deep breath. Did she want something more with him? Yes, she couldn't fool herself into thinking differently. Was she actually falling for him? She didn't know —at least not yet.

She sat there contemplating their relationship and what it meant to her while Bernard sat at her side and waited patiently for one more chase of the stick.

Aaron had been working for days on the kitchen, and it

was coming along quite nicely. Most of the cabinets were up and some of the walls were even painted. As he finished painting another wall, he stood back, rolled his shoulders and took stock of his work.

He had sweat rolling down his back; his energy was quickly draining. Taking a swallow of cool water, he decided it was time for a break. Instead of a walk to the pond, he felt the beach was beckoning him. He could use the cold wind in his face to clear his mind of work and Lacey, which lately, seemed to dominate his waking thoughts.

He realized he was getting used to his walks in the forest. And this time, he enjoyed taking the long narrow path that lead to the rocky shore of the ocean. He was wondering how he had ever relaxed in the city, without getting out in nature.

He was enjoying the sounds of the waves crashing ashore violently as he started across the wide clearing of sand. His wondering was interrupted by a dog barking in the clearing and then he caught sight of Lacey sitting on a log, watching the sunset. Sidetracking across the stretch of beach, he walked towards them.

He was half way to the log when the dog caught sight of him and ran towards him. Bernard's ears were flying in the cold breeze and he had a huge stick in his mouth. Aaron was positive the dog was smiling.

Lacey had made no movement and seemed deep in thought until Aaron threw Bernard's stick over her head. She jumped up and looked guilty, but then she rose and started walking towards him. He loved the way she walked; her strides seemed to quickly eat up the ground between them.

How could someone so small walk so fast?

He'd enjoyed seeing her at the grocery store a few days earlier, and as he watched her march up to him, he realized he wanted to rile her up again. However, his desires might have to be put on hold, as it appeared Lacey had something on her mind.

Her face was set with determination, and when she stopped her hands went to her hips.

"Why is it, Dr. Stevens, that wherever I am, there you are?" she asked, a little out of breath from the quick walk across the wet sand.

She looked like she could have walked out of the sea herself; her face was flush, and her short hair was blowing frantically as she waited for a reply.

Tonight, she wore a bright green jacket, black leggings, and a pair of old brown boots. He could make out a pair of bright green socks with frogs on them, poking out from the above the boots. The darkness of her outfit accented the color of her and the beauty of her face.

Her lips pouted when he didn't reply fast enough, making Aaron smile. He closed the rest of the distance between them and pulled her close. He could hear her breath catch and saw anger flash in her eyes.

"What do you think you are doing?" she asked, trying to pull away. "I am not a play thing for you to paw." She got no further, as his mouth claimed hers.

After her head stopped spinning, she realized her hands were gripping his shoulders. She couldn't believe it. Here he was walking on her beach. Damn it all, what was the man doing on her beach? Was no place of hers sacred, anymore?

He shifted his head for a better angle, which allowed her to wrap her arms around his shoulders.

Bernard was happily running around them in circles as Aaron kissed every last drop of anger from her body.

She could still smell the water, but now she could also smell him. He smelled of sawdust and paint. Why did she find that sexy? How was she supposed to stay mad with a man who could kiss her like this?

His lips softened, and his warm body moved closer as his hands roamed up and down her back, sending sweet waves of desire coursing throughout all of her limbs.

As she ran her hands through his hair, she felt him shudder and a feeling of power, and desire, raced through her.

Was she trying to kill him? He knew he'd started it and he'd thought that he could keep himself in check. But now he could swear she was the one in control. A soft sweet moan escaped her lips, which sent chills coursing throughout his entire body.

He ran his hands up and down her spine and felt her melt against him. Maybe neither of them was in control?

He reached under her jacket and felt her warm soft skin.

"Please," she said when he ran his mouth down her long neck. He was enjoying the soft taste of her ear lobe, nibbling on the sweetness of it.

"Please what? Tell me what you want," he asked as he continued kissing her neck. He couldn't stop shaking as she ran her hands over his shoulders and grabbed his hair and pulled his mouth back to her own.

He came back to reality when he felt her stiffen as he attempted to pull her jacket away.

What is wrong with me? wondered Lacey. Was she destined to lose all control every time she was around this man? She felt the cold wind on her back and felt his warm hands on her skin. To be honest with herself, she didn't want to stop. She could imagine making love to Aaron, here in the cold sand, on her beach, under the stars.

"I can't, I just can't. Please Aaron, let me go." She looked into his eyes and could see that they were still clouded with desire.

She was sure a physical relationship with him would be pure pleasure, but she truly wanted more. She was not sure at this moment what she really wanted and until she was, she needed more time to think.

"Games again, Lacey?" He smiled down at her, trying to make light of the fact that he was still not in control of himself.

He felt and saw the change building in her and pulled back before he got scorched.

"I'm sorry, I didn't mean that," he said.

"I don't know who you think you are," she started, and pulled herself away to sit down on the log again.

She tucked her knees close to her body with her arms wrapped around them tightly. "I don't play games. You follow me around and paw at me in front of everyone."

"Wait a minute, Lacey," he said as he sat down next to her, running his hands through his hair. "I haven't been following you around like some sort of dog." With these words, Bernard set his paw on Aaron's knees.

"You must think very highly of yourself, if you believe that." He tried to keep his anger in check.

She saw the truth in his eyes and instantly felt sorry that she could accuse him of something so stupid. But then what did she really know about him? Oh, she knew about his type and had made a point of staying clear of men like Aaron. She glanced over at him as he struggled with his anger and her wet dog. He was easy enough to get along with, but he had yet to open himself up to her. Did she really want just a physical relationship with him or was there something more?

"Listen Aaron, I'm sorry, I've had a lot on my mind and I don't know what to make of you, yet." She reached down and threw Bernard's stick to relieve Aaron of the wet doggie paws.

"One minute you're setting me on fire and the next you're cold as ice and going out of your way to piss me off." She ran her hand through her hair in displeasure. "Can we start over and try to be friends?" She watched his eyes focus on her face and then saw the quick smile which started in his eyes.

"No, Lacey, I can't just be your friend. I think we both know we want more than friendship." He leaned over and gave her another quick kiss that had her toes curling.

Quickly, he stood up and pulled her up after him. "Come on, I'll walk you two home."

CHAPTER 7

The house was going to kill him, he thought, after hitting his fingers, elbows, knees, and his head multiple times. He would have thought he had suffered enough for the place, but no. Now the "Beast," as he liked to call it, had taken a chunk out of his pride and made him feel stupid.

Why couldn't he figure out the damn electrical wires? He had aced medical school...aced it! So why couldn't he figure out where the damned green wire was supposed to be connected? Aaron sat looking at his recently purchased book, *Home Wiring for Dummies,* and thought he might as well be looking at a schematic for the space shuttle. There were pages loaded with black, white, and red wire information, but nothing – nothing! – on green wires.

Looking down at the lone green wire in his hand, he started to question whether he was color blind. Did color blind people see red as green? He had always assumed they saw everything in gray scales, kind of like dogs.

He'd been here almost four months now and had worked on the house almost every night, as well as putting in a full day at the office five days a week. Maybe he needed a break from working? Maybe it was just him?

Frustrated, he tossed the book across the empty floor and decided to call a local electrician tomorrow.

He knew that heavy gossip was rolling through town, especially after he kissed Lacey in front of the grocery store. He'd heard the gossip at the hardware store, the grocery store, and even in his damn office. He could tell that every eye was on him, whenever he drove through town. Maybe a break from the town was needed?

He was sure every woman from at least two counties had come in to the office over the last few months, wanting in on the gossip. Every woman except the one he couldn't get his mind off.

After putting in a full nine hours at the office and spending the last two hours hunched over the wires poking out of his bare walls, he needed a break, a beer, and a woman.

Stalking out of the room, he grabbed his coat, and decided a cold walk on the beach would clear his mind.

Maybe he would see Lacey there again?

He headed down the narrow path that led to the beach, his mind racing. He really enjoyed the solitude of the place, the peace and quiet of the small town, not to mention the friendly people—people so much unlike what he had ever experienced before.

As he made his way toward the beach he realized that no one from his old life, except for Jennifer, had tried to contact him after the large scene that had played out at that last party. Shuttering, he tried not to think about the terrible night.

He continued to think about it as the trail head opened up to the cold windy beach. He'd made a point to avoid any and all calls from Jennifer, even at the hospital. He had to tell the nurses and staff not to page him every time she called.

He looked out at the water and walked down to the water's edge. Hearing the gulls calling out their sad song as the cold salt water sprayed his face, he realized he had never felt more alive.

He had walked around life in a daze for a few weeks after that party. Looking back at it now, he was sure it was his grandfather's call that had woke him up. After that, he had quickly packed up his life. A week later he was a home owner and living just down the street from some of the nicest people he had ever known.

Thinking about the Jordan's, he doubted that any of them would have walked away from a friend in need. He picked up a pebble to throw into the surf and smiled as he thought of Lacey. Somehow the cold air and the salt water hitting his face didn't seem so cold anymore.

———

THREE DAYS later he stood and watched others work around his house for the first time in over four months.

The place was definitely coming along now. He had several walls painted, had hired a plumber to put in the shower and toilets, and an electrician to finish the small things that frankly annoyed him.

He hadn't seen or heard from Lacey in over a week. Every time he'd traveled down to the restaurant, she was nowhere to be found. How could she avoid him in such a small town?

The electrician, John Timothy, walked up interrupting his thoughts. John was a big man in his late fifties, with shoulders and hands like boulders, but he had a smile that told of his easy personality. Aaron liked the guy immediately.

"We can have you all set up today; shouldn't take my guys much longer. Be out of here around four."

"Great." Aaron shook hands with him. "I can't tell you how grateful I am." Aaron shuddered remembering the electrical book that was now in the bottom of one of the trash cans outside. "I should be back around three or so. You have my number in case you have any questions?"

"Sure do. It's a pleasure having you here in town. Your granddad helped deliver my four boys; course they're all grown up now," he said with a big smile, nodding towards two of the workers. "They help me out these days."

"You must be proud," he smiled back.

"Oh, I am. You're doing a great job fixing this old place up. It used to be a real looker, and from the looks of it, will be again."

"Thank you."

"Course a house this size needs a family to fill it. You a family man, Mr. Stevens?"

Aaron smiled, "No, but I would like to be." He'd heard this question countless times over the last few months. Now it seemed to him all he had ever wanted in his life was a family...a real family. That is what he'd been searching for when he'd run into Jennifer.

Looking back now, he thought she had exploited his weakness of wanting a family and home. But as his thought turned to family, it wasn't Jennifer's face that came into view. Instead of the tall busty blonde, a petite raven-haired beauty came into focus. Shaking his head, he figured another stop at The Golden Oar after work couldn't hurt him. And if Lacey wasn't there, then he would have a quick talk with her brother, Iian, and see where she had been hiding herself.

As it happened, she wasn't there. But Iian was and he was heading to the boys and girls club to play a game of basketball with a group of guys he'd been playing with since grade school. Of course, he had invited Aaron along, and Aaron quickly agreed. Maybe beating some locals in a sport, which he kicked butt in would help level him out.

What he hadn't expected was to get his butt handed back to him, bruised and beaten. How could a bunch of small town guys play so hard and viciously? Iian was one of the worst offenders; Aaron was fouled more times than he could count, and he had ended up on the ground more than he wanted to. No doubt, he would be black and blue with bruises tomorrow.

"Where did you guys learn to be that ruthless?" Aaron signed to Iian as they changed in the locker room.

"People think I'll take it easy on them, or that I can't play well because of my hearing," Iian signed back. "I played all throughout middle and high school." He picked up his shoes and tossed them in his locker, then shut it. Then he continued, "If you think we play rough, you should see my sister and those hoodlums they call middle graders. She coaches girls basketball and softball in the spring and summer for the B&G club."

"Lacey plays basketball?" He thought of Lacey jumping at the hoop and wondered how high she could jump. He had thought about putting up a hoop at his place, but now he knew he wanted to get one up first thing next spring.

Iian laughed, then signed, "Even though she's short, the little girl can jump."

The pair laughed as they left the gym.

TAKING TIME OUT, was something everyone needed to do, at least once a week. Lacey enjoyed floating in her pond in the warmer parts of the year, but once the weather turned cold, she took to the pool at the Boys and Girls club. She enjoyed being at the club so much that she had signed up to teach young kids how to swim.

Thinking about that decision on the drive into town, she now wondered if she had lost her mind.

Why did she think she had enough time to do this? Why would she put herself through this sort of punishment? Was there aspirin in the car for afterwords? Did she still really want five kids herself?

All these questions raced through her mind until she saw the little faces waiting by the side of the pool. Boys and girls above the age of five sat on the edge of the club's smaller pool. Some of the smaller kids wore floating devices; the others were skilled or old enough to not need the help.

"Hello, Miss Jordan," the kids said in unison.

"Hello, everyone. Who's ready to learn the breaststroke today?"

Upon hearing the word 'breaststroke' all the kids started giggling.

This was the reason she taught once a week; the smiles and laughter of the young children in her town could never be replaced. Lacey's week felt complete.

CHAPTER 8

*L*acey had been avoiding Aaron again. She was sure she would run into him sooner or later, she just preferred it to be later. It had been a little over a week since she'd seen him last and she knew he was keeping busy up at the house. She was keeping busy herself.

As she waited on a table of twelve, nine of whom were children under the age of ten, she thought of how she'd seen him several times around town. She had made a point to always be heading in the opposite direction.

What had he meant when he said he wanted more than friendship? She could only guess what she thought he meant, but every time she went over it in her mind she started to question his motives. Was she ready for something more with Aaron?

She couldn't get over the feelings he had stirred up in her. She'd never felt anything like this before. She'd had a few boy friends in high school and since, but she'd never really taken a relationship serious before. Every time she thought about Aaron, her toes started to tingle. It could be that she was having low blood sugar due to the fact that she'd pulled several hours of overtime and hadn't stopped to eat all that much. All she had to show for it was a blister on her right heel from working too much.

She thought that if she kept busy she wouldn't have time to think about what had almost happened between them. Last night, she'd gotten home at one in the morning only to pick up the early shift again. Another double shift day lay ahead of her.

Setting down the menus, she saw the three moms were doing their best to ignore the fact that their table was the loudest spot in town. She recognized two of the women from her school days. She remembered they hadn't run in the same crowd as her; she had been somewhat of a loner. But she remembered their names, Stacie and Bridget.

She started the kid's drink order and noticed that their mothers' heads stayed bent over a small book that held pictures. When she asked them for their drink order, she noticed that both women had changed since school. It appeared they were very comfortable with their lives because each had gained about thirty pounds.

Both ordered diet drinks without even glancing at her. Lacey went to fill their drink order and delivered food to two more tables before heading back to ask for their food orders.

"Has everyone decided what they would like for lunch today?" Lacey leaned down and put a small blonde girl back in her chair before she hit the floor.

"Oh, yes, well…" Stacie began looking over her menu at Lacey. "You went to school with us, didn't you?" Lacey noted how she had chosen to word the question, as if it had been a privilege to attend the same educational facility as the great Stacie and Bridget.

"Yes, we were in the same grade. Have you decided on your food order?" Lacey had no problem conversing with most of the people she went to school with but didn't care to with the two girls who had caused her some pain during those awkward years.

"Lizzy, or Libby, isn't that your name?" Bridget smiled over to Stacie. Lacey had the feeling they both knew her name.

"Lacey," she said, pointing to her name tag pinned to her shirt. "Have you decided?" Lacey pulled out her pad and patiently waited.

Lacey remembered they both had crushes on Todd and Iian during junior high and senior high school. She also remembered that at one point the duo had decided to bring Lacey into their little circle, with the hopes they would get to spend time over at her house. Probably fishing to obtain one of the two most sought-after brothers in town.

"Lacey, that's it. Aren't you Iian and Todd's sister?" Bridget jumped in smiling.

Of the two, Bridget was the one that Lacey despised the most. Bridget had moved away from Pride after graduation and Lacey knew she'd married a lawyer in Portland. Stacie had stayed in town and married the high school quarterback, who now worked across the river at a mill. Lacey still didn't travel in the circles they did; actually, she made a point to stay clear of them.

Lacey nodded and knew she'd be unable to take their orders until they had played out their game. She might as well go along with it.

"So you're still working here, how quaint. I was just talking to Stacie about this place the other day. I haven't been back into town since I moved to Portland. I can't believe the old place is still standing. We decided to take the kids for a ride down memory lane. These are my four here, two boys and two girls. Stacie has three boys there and this is our friend, Beth, along with her two girls." Bridget nodded to the two girls at the table who were sitting quietly coloring on the kids' menus. Of all the children, Lacey noticed the best behaved of the children didn't belong to either Stacie or Bridget.

Lacey looked at the small woman whose blonde hair was pulled back in a neat braid that reached down the middle of her back. She had a polite smile on her face and appeared to be embarrassed by the rudeness of her two friends.

Lacey returned the smile. "Nice to meet you, Beth. I'm Lacey Jordan, owner of the Golden Oar. Welcome." Both Stacie and Bridget let out dual breaths that sounded more like hissing.

"You have beautiful girls. Have you two decided what you want to eat?" Lacey leaned over and saw that the girls were drawing with crayons, trying to mimic the painting of the green mermaid on the opposite wall. Their little blonde heads were bent together as if they were trying to keep out all of the loud noises from the children who were currently running around the table screaming.

She smiled at the pair. "My grandmother drew that picture years ago; you girls have some talent."

"Thank you," both girls said in unison, with eyes wide open at Lacey.

The older girl ordered her meal followed by the younger, then Lacey took everyone else's order.

When she was done taking orders, the smallest of Beth's girls pulled on her apron.

"See, I drew'd you." Lacey bent down next to the girl. She saw what she assumed was a copy of her grandmother's mermaid and next to the figure was a Pixie with purple wings.

"Why, that looks just like me. Good job!" she smiled.

A half an hour later, Lacey walked back into the kitchen. Her feet hurt and her head hurt. The headache began when

Stacie started talking about the new hunk doctor that had moved into town and how she'd set appointments for all of her kids just to get a better look at him. Lacey tried to avoid listening in, but Stacie had such a big mouth she could barely hear herself think over her voice.

Two hours later, she no longer had a headache; instead her head felt like it was going to explode. The place was packed with mothers and their screaming kids. Apparently, it had been the last day of school before the Thanksgiving break, so everyone within two counties had decided to come into the Golden Oar to eat.

Lacey even called for backup and had hastily promoted Katie from greeter to waiting tables. Katie was a hard worker and deserved the promotion. Plus, she had been working at the restaurant for almost two years, so she knew all the ropes.

It took seven more wait staff and two more hours to clear the place out. They had about four hours before they needed to start getting ready for the dinner rush.

Lacey sat at an empty table with a soft drink and some aspirin; she didn't think she would make it through the evening shift. Her head was getting worse; her vision was narrowing as if looking through a tunnel. What really bothered her was remembering Stacie and Bridget giggling over the new town doctor, Stacie and Aaron…Aaron and Stacie.

She was leaning back with her eyes closed trying to decide whether she was going to be mad or sick when she heard a loud crash in the kitchen followed by screaming.

Running into the kitchen, she saw Katie sitting in a chair; Iian was holding her head down between her legs. She had a towel wrapped around her hand which Iian held above her head. Lacey saw the blood.

Rushing over, she grabbed a fresh towel and began to apply pressure to the wound, while trying to calm the girl down. When she'd glimpsed the wound, she knew the girl would need stitches. Looking up at Iian, he nodded in silent agreement. Katie was very pale, but Lacey could see her eyes were still clear and focused.

"Katie, I'm going to drive you over to the doctor's office, so he can have a look at this. Can you walk?"

When she nodded, they helped her into Lacey's car for the short drive. Lacey kept Katie calm by talking to her about the busy lunch hour they'd had. When she pulled up to the door, Aaron came rushing out with a wheel chair.

"The restaurant called ahead," Aaron said, helping Katie into the wheel chair. "How are you feeling, Katie?" Aaron started to wheel Katie into the building and down the hall while asking her questions, to keep her alert. Not once did he look over at Lacey.

Lacey was left standing in the doorway holding a bloody towel.

She hadn't been into the office since Aaron had taken over the practice. She noticed there was new paint and carpet and the old hardwood floors had been refurnished. Lacey walked into what used to be Dr. Steven's office; it had been turned into a waiting room with new leather couches. A flat-screen TV sat in the corner and a small table with boxes of toys sat underneath. Along one wall was a huge fish tank with tropical fish swimming around peacefully. This was a doctor's office. Oh, it had always been a doctor's office, just not this...shiny.

Lacey let out the breath she'd been holding for too long and sat on one of the new couches to stare at the door, waiting for Aaron to walk in.

AARON'S HEART had skipped a beat when he'd heard that one

of the girls at the restaurant had cut her hand pretty bad. The boy who had called hadn't known the details, only that someone had been hurt and they were being driven over. When he had seen Lacey's car pull up, panic had surged through him. Then Lacey had gotten out of the car and he noticed Katie sitting in the passenger seat, holding her hand above her head.

As he put little stitches into the palm of Katie's left hand, he allowed her to chat about the busy day at the restaurant. He'd given her a local anesthetic and could see the color finally coming back into her cheeks.

When he finished and was wrapping her hand up in gauze, a short stout woman came rushing in.

"Katie? Oh my God! Doctor, is she going to lose her hand?"

"No ma'am, she just needed a few stitches. She cut it pretty deep, so I'll prescribe an antibiotic along with pain pills. She'll need to keep the bandages dry and clean for a week."

Aaron walked the two women out of his office with assurances that the hand wasn't going to need to be amputated. He stood in the doorway watching them leave and noticed Lacey's car was still sitting in front of the building.

He walked back to the waiting room and saw her curled up on the couch clutching a blood-stained towel, fast asleep.

Walking over to a closet, he pulled out a medical blanket and covered her up. He slid the towel out of her fist and noticed that she didn't move. Bending down, he could see the lines under her eyes. He had been focused on his patient before and hadn't had time to look at Lacey other than to make sure she was not the one bleeding. But now that he did look at her, he could clearly see she had not been getting enough sleep.

She looked so small curled up on his waiting room couch.

Brushing a strand of dark hair from her forehead, he leaned down and placed a light kiss on her temple.

He was closing up, but now stood and headed back to his office, figuring he would catch up on some of the paperwork he had been putting off. He would call over to make sure Iian knew that Katie was fine, and that Lacey needed the rest of the night off.

COLORS FLOODED Lacey's mind along with a warm soft feeling that surrounded her senses. She felt warm strong arms wrap around her, and she turned into them with a sigh. She had to be dreaming.

Then memory came to her and she remembered about Katie and her injury. Her eyes flew open and she saw the waiting room. She was in strong arms, but it wasn't a dream.

Looking up at Aaron she asked, "What do you think you're doing?"

"You say that a lot. Do you always wake up in such a hurry?" he smiled down at her. His whole face was lit up and his eyes sparkled.

She was nestled in his arms with her head on his strong shoulders. She was so close to his face that she noticed a freckle on the left side of his forehead. She fought the urge to reach up and touch it.

"Where is Katie? Is she going to be okay? What happened? And why are you carrying me?" she asked as she started squirming in his arms.

"She's fine, her mother came and took her home. You, on the other hand, are not fine. You fell asleep, and from the look of it, you haven't been getting enough of it lately."

He walked down the hall and out the back door. He tried to lock the door while keeping Lacey tight in his grip.

"If you put me down, it'll be easier to lock the door," she said, giving up her struggle to wiggle her way out of his hold.

"Nope, can't, I like the feel of you too much." He shifted her weight and successfully locked the door. "There! See? I got it." Then he proceeded to carry her towards his new silver truck.

"Where are you taking me? My car is over there," she said, pointing towards her sedan.

"Well, let's see, because you've gone out of your way to avoid me the last couple of weeks, I figured we have some catching up to do. So, I'm taking you someplace to eat."

"I have not been avoiding you," she said, crossing her arms and staring up at him. "And I can't go to dinner with you; I have to get back to work."

"No," Aaron leaned over. He opened the truck door then placed her on the front seat gently, but unceremoniously.

"What do you mean, no?" She was so shocked at the simple statement, she didn't think about getting back out of the truck. She sat there and watched as he walked around the hood.

"I mean no, you're not going back to work tonight. I called and told them you needed the rest of the night off," he said, as he got into the driver's side of the truck.

"You did what?" she said, as she began to get out of the truck.

"Don't, I'll just put you right back in." The look he gave her confirmed he would do just that.

"You have no right," she began.

"You don't want to mess with me now, Lacey," he said quietly, which stopped her. She looked over at him.

It wasn't so much the words that stopped her; it was the calm manner in which he had spoken.

"Please," he whispered. The simple word made her change her mind more than anything.

Crossing her arms over her chest again, she sat back while he drove. She did not really see where they were headed because she was too deep in thought about his words, the emotions behind them, and what they might mean.

By the time the truck stopped, her eyes had shut once more. Aaron walked around and picked her up again. She didn't fight him this time; instead she let out a small moan and then up to his chest.

At that moment, he knew he was in deep. He stood there for a moment while this feeling sank in. He could hear her breath and feel her warmth against his arms. Finally, he turned and walked into an empty house. Walking into his home all alone was one thing but carrying a sleeping woman was a completely different event.

After he placed her gently on his new king bed, he looked down at her as she snuggled into the soft pillow top and murmured something inaudible.

He gently tugged off her shoes and smiled at the bright yellow socks. He leaned down closer and realized the socks were covered in turkeys, which made him smile even more.

He brushed her hair away from her face. What a face it was. He liked how he could read every emotion that crossed into her eyes.

He could tell others were baffled by her, but he'd figured out how to tell her moods; earlier in the car he knew she was upset, but also knew that she was suffering from lack of sleep and a headache. It was like a story that he could read in her eyes—tired eyes which hadn't shown tonight like all the other times, he had seen her.

He turned off the lights and closed the door before walking down his half-finished hallway. He realized Jennifer hadn't been easy to read, but their relationship had been based on a physical attraction. He had failed to listen to his heart and in the end, he had paid for it.

He hadn't thought it would be possible to ever recover from what that woman had done to him.

Walking into the kitchen, he enjoyed the feel of the place. His newly purchased appliances were all hooked up and humming, making the place seem more alive. He could picture the final product. He still had to finish painting, finish some of the flooring, and there were still some fixtures left to hang. Then he could start on the yard and the deck he planned on building out back.

Walking to the back of the house, he thought he would get started on the first real dinner in this house. He was glad Lacey would be here to share in the experience.

As he started dinner preparations, he realized he knew he would be able to trust Lacey. This was someone who was honest and caring. He liked the whole Jordan clan for that matter. For the first time in his life, he felt like he belonged somewhere. In the short time he'd been part of this small community, he truly felt like he fit in.

CHAPTER 9

The heavenly aroma drifted into her sleeping mind, causing her stomach to growl. Turning over in the bed, she tried to ignore the persistent hunger pains.

Then in a flash she was sitting up and looking around the strange room. The light in the room was too dim to really see anything other than shapes, so she searched for a lamp and flicked it on.

The room was huge with the king-sized bed sitting in the center. There were no pictures on the unpainted walls and, she noted, there were no doors.

She realized she was in Aaron's place, in his bedroom to be exact. After her initial shock she became curious and really looked around. Large glass doors covered one wall that might look out to the back yard. A chest of drawers with a small flat screen sat on another wall and next to it there was another doorway.

She walked to the doorway and flipped on the light to reveal a very large bathroom. The walls were a warm blue, and there was a glass shower, an inviting bath tub, and double sinks. The whole place gleamed and shined. She could see the closet off the other end of the room and turned back into the bedroom to find the source of the wonderful smells.

There was a short unfinished hallway covered with papers. At first, she thought they were plans for the house. As she approached them she realized they were drawings from children. There must have been a dozen taped on the unpainted drywall.

She leaned closer to one drawing and saw a multicolored rainbow arched around a small figure with a red cast arm and, another larger figure with a white coat on. She read the uneven print *"Thanks, Dr. Stevens, for fixing my hurt arm with my favorite color. Evan."*

She moved to another that showed a small girl with a big bandage on her face. A man sat next to her holding a small bunny, which also had a bandage on its face. It read, *"Thank you for helping Lela and me. Love Jenny."*

She read them all, taking her time to make sure she knew each child. She didn't realize it, but silent tears had dripped down her cheeks as she read.

This man had come into her town, had fixed up this broken-down house, and one of the first things he hung up, so that he would pass them every day, were pictures the town children had drawn for him.

But what had caused the tears and made her heart to break was the picture at the end of the hallway. The wall was blank; it's freshly painted cream color accented the one picture in a dark cherry frame. Inside sat two circled faces, one with blue eyes and another with brown. Both faces had matching smiles and noses. One had blonde hair and the other dark. Tommy Thomas had only been six when he was diagnosed with Leukemia. It had been a hard blow to the small town of Pride and an even harder blow when he had lost the battle a month ago. The last few days of his life had been filled with town members fulfilling every wish the little boy had ever had.

Stepping closer to the picture, she remembered the party the town had to celebrate his last birthday.

However, looking at this drawing opened a spot in her heart she hadn't ever touched before. Through her wet eyes she could see Tommy and Aaron smiling, and realized the joy shared between a child and his friend, the doctor. It was a friendship that appeared to mean as much to the doctor as it had to the child.

Knowing Aaron had taken the time to frame the child's picture and hang it in a place of honor in his home helped her realize her feelings for him were something she couldn't set aside anymore. She knew deep down that this man, who filled his home with the drawings from children that weren't his own, had stolen her heart.

Her eyes became unfocused as she realized she was in love. How had it come to this? The man infuriated her. Didn't he? She had tried to ignore him and ignore her feelings for him. But now all these pictures had shattered the lock, around her heart that had been holding her back from the last big leap.

Taking a deep breath, she shook her head and chuckled. Wasn't it just like her to fall in love with a man who would keep her on her toes? Well, she was sure of one thing; life would not be boring. All that was left was to convince him he couldn't live without her.

Confident now in her new-found emotions, she continued exploring the house and arrived in what she would consider the great room. The room took up half the house and held a leather couch, a cherry coffee table, and a flat screen television next to a huge stone fireplace. She noticed that there was not much else in the room; there weren't pictures or mementos here.

Aaron had left the ceiling high, with the wood trusses exposed. They were stained a dark color and gave the room an open feeling. She could see all the way to the backside of the house and looked into the kitchen through a large opening in one wall. Heading back towards the delicious smells, she noticed that Aaron's back was to her while he chopped something. Lacey leaned against the wall and crossed her arms over her chest and continued to look around.

The house had come a long way since she'd been there last. The kitchen was beyond breathtaking. She estimated that it was larger than her own and was full of new appliances. She smiled when she saw the stove was restaurant quality and gas to boot! The man knew how to put a kitchen together.

Where most of the rest of the house still needed painting, wall coverings, and furniture, the kitchen seemed to be complete.

She noted that the cabinets were a dark cherry and the counters were marble. She approved of the dark wood blinds that hung in the windows along with the island that cut the room in two. She wanted to take a look at the stacked ovens that stood on the opposite wall, and then spotted the glass door refrigerator, completely stocked with food. I guess he can feed himself now, she thought.

Just then Aaron turned around and was startled to see her standing there, causing him to almost drop the hand full of onions he had chopped.

"Oh! You're awake." He smiled, trying for a smooth recovery.

"Mmm, smells good." She leaned over and took a carrot off a plate.

"I like what you've done with the place." Walking over she ran her hand on the smooth counter top and rounded the island to sit on one of the bar stools. Placing her chin in her hand, she watched him dump the onions into a sizzling pan.

"Hope you don't mind fish. My grandfather caught these." He smiled as he placed another fish filet in the pan then glanced over at her when she did not answer. "You seem surprised that I can cook," he said after noticing her expression.

"A doctor and a cook? What else have you got up your sleeves?" She shrugged as she started to nibble on the carrot.

"Hmm, I give a mean massage." When he smiled over at her, she fought the urge to blush.

He watched her lips as she ate the carrot and was transfixed by her mouth. She was killing him. He almost forgot to keep an eye on the fish.

When he turned back to the stove, she finished the carrot and stretched her arms above her head. "I guess I was more tired than I thought."

"I'm glad you got some rest; it's not healthy to work yourself like that." He paused as he flipped the filets. "You know, if you wanted to avoid me, you could have simply stayed home." Looking over his shoulder, he realized he hit the mark by the guilty look she gave him.

"Listen, Aaron…" she started.

"Please don't. Let's just enjoy a nice civilized dinner," he said, changing gears. He removed the fish from the heat.

She felt the urge to explain more but went with the mood. "Sure, can I help?"

"No, tonight I serve you. Go on into the dining room." He pointed her towards another room off the side of the kitchen. "I'll bring this right in."

Lacey walked into the next room and smiled. It was smaller than the kitchen, but very comfortable. Huge picture windows covered one wall and, in the middle, stood a circular cherry table with four cushioned chairs. To the side stood a small dinette, and a fire crackled in the stone fire-place on the opposite wall. Above the fire was a picture. She walked closer and saw it was a painting of a ship set on storming waters. She smiled when she saw it had been painted by her friend Allison, who owned an antique shop in town.

She saw wine chilling on the side table and candles set on the table. She moved to light them and was pleased by their jasmine smell. Aaron had good taste. He walked in carrying a salad and after setting it on the table, he walked back out. She noted there were almonds and green olives among the fresh leaves and had to smile. Okay, he had really good taste.

Dinner was excellent, and the conversation some of the best, she had enjoyed in a long time.

"You know, we could use another chef down at the restaurant," she said later as she helped him clear the table.

"No, thank you, I like my profession." Grabbing the plates from her, he nodded towards a bar stool. He then proceeded to carry the dishes to the sink and started rinsing them.

"Where did you learn to cook?" she asked as she finished off her glass of wine.

"Here and there, but mainly in Paris. I was there for about a year." He noticed her glass was empty and filled it for the third time. He could see that the wine had dulled the headache, he had noticed earlier in her eyes.

"Really, Paris? I lived there, too," she smiled.

"I went through this phase in my life and I thought Paris was the answer." A small crease crossed his forehead.

"I went there to find myself," she said, smiling over at him. "That's where I met Matt, Megan's brother. You could say he came to my rescue when a date went bad." She smiled again, remembering the night.

"You met Matt, in Paris?" Aaron felt a stab of jealousy. He knew that Matt had died recently, but it got him wondering whether there had been something between her and Megan's brother.

"Yes." She saw the look that came into his eyes and did not mind the pleasure it caused her to see he was a little jealous. "I had met this painter – yes, I know, it's a cliché – but he had these big puppy dog eyes and spoke with the sexiest Spanish accent and he asked me to pose for his drawings."

Aaron let out a breath that sounded a lot like a laugh.

"What?" she asked tilting her head.

"You didn't really fall for that line, did you?" he asked, sipping his wine as he leaned against the counter. He looked very relaxed and sexy in the cozy kitchen.

"Oh, it was no line." She smiled into her wine. "Naturally when he invited me to meet him later that afternoon at the café down the street, I saw no harm in it."

"And he jumped at you?" Aaron could see where this was going and didn't like it.

"Oh no, we had a lovely time. He was a shy and quiet gentleman and a very good artist. I still have the painting hanging in my bedroom." She smiled again.

Aaron realized his hands were clenched around his wine glass, so he forced his fingers to relax.

"Where does Matt come into the picture?"

"Well, you see, I met Ricardo at the café to pick up my painting, and while you would never think it to look at him, he was married with four children. I guess his wife didn't like the attention he had been giving me, so she showed up at the café, to his surprise."

Aaron drew a breath trying to be patient, but he was having a hard time. Apparently when Lacey told a story, the details were very important.

"Well, as luck would have it, Matt had overheard the ensuing argument as he was sitting at the next table. When Mrs. Ricardo was threatening to scratch my eyes out, Matt jumped in and explained, in Spanish no less, that he had commissioned Ricardo to paint me for a wedding anniversary present. Then he quickly paid for the piece of art and we left the café together." Lacey smiled again thinking the whole thing was just as funny now. as it had been then.

"Matt was a great friend." She stopped smiling and looked sad. "We spent weeks together exploring Paris, and when he found out I was from Pride, I guess he decided to come for a visit. Turns out he had been born near here and came to visit when his trip to Paris was over."

Remembering the fond times, she had with her friend before his death, she took a deep breath.

Wanting to change the subject, she stood up and started to walk around the room. "You really have gotten a lot done around here. That kitchen is something else." Her headache was dull, and she thought she was a little tipsy, but she enjoyed the feeling. He followed her into the next room and listened to her as she explored the rooms.

"You amaze me." The simple statement made her do a double take as she was inspecting the fireplace in the great room.

"I... I do? Why?"

"Because you see the good in people, you're not out for self-gain, and you trust people easily. I'm worried you're going to get hurt someday." He took her wine glass and set it on the coffee table and walked back over to her.

"I don't trust everyone." It was a whisper in the large room. She felt very much like the mouse waiting for the cat to pounce. Taking a deep breath, she took a step back and tumbled onto the couch she had not realized was behind her.

Aaron chuckled then sat next to her.

"Do I make you nervous?" he asked, as he leaned over and placed his arm around her to pull her closer to him.

"Yes, dreadfully so. Why then do you do that?" she asked, looking over at him.

He gently smoothed the crease in her brow with the back of his finger, then let his fingers trail down her face and settle under her chin. Nudging her face up, he looked into her eyes and realized she was more than a little drunk. Her cheeks were flushed, and her eyes were slightly out of focus, but her lips looked very inviting.

"You inspire me." He leaned down and tasted her mouth. He meant to show her tenderness, but the taste of her and the feel of her sent him spinning. Pulling her closer so that she almost sat on his lap, he reached around and gripped her hips.

Her hands were already racing over his face and neck to tangle in his hair. She nipped at his lips, gave a quick tug, and then smoothed the sting away with her tongue. She pushed him back to the couch and straddled him. She pinned his back to the cushions to deepen the kiss.

She was driving him mad and he let her. He hadn't brought her here tonight to seduce her; he had just been concerned. When he found her asleep on his office couch, he had been angry at her for letting herself get in that kind of state. As a doctor he knew the importance of rest and maintaining your own health; she needed to take better care of herself. She needed someone to help her and he was going to. But now she felt good. Her soft body was pushed up against his as he enjoyed feeling her rapid heartbeat. He skimmed his hands up her back and started to pull her shirt up to trace the contours with his fingertips.

She pulled back as she leaned over him and looked down into his eyes.

"I wasn't going to do this, you know," he said, continuing to toy with her soft skin and looking up at her with confusion.

"I've waited and waited. I never thought it would be with someone like you." She said, starting to lean down to take his mouth again, but felt his body tense. She looked down into his face and saw fear. Laughing, she grabbed her sides and flopped onto the couch next to him.

"You think this is funny?" he said, pulling himself up and running his hands through his hair and giving it a good yank to try to bring some sense into his brain.

"Yes. You stalk me for months and then at one hint at my innocence, you freak out and can't speak." She laughed again at the look he gave her. "I'm a virgin, not an alien."

"Lacey, this is serious," he began, sitting back up. "I…" He looked at her, "I…" He ran his hands roughly through his hair again, mentally pulling it all out by the roots. What was he supposed to do? She sat across from him with her mouth swollen from his lips, her work shirt, which was always so neat and proper, pulled from her waist band and tugged to one side, and she was laughing like a loon. Her laugh was rich and smoky and only caused more desire to spread within him.

How could he do this? She was innocent!

Seeing his frustrations, she leaned in and kissed him on the nose and placed her fingers on his chin, pulling his face to hers.

"Lacey, I don't want to pressure you." He ran his hands up and down her arms as she straddled him again.

"The only pressure I feel now, I know you can relieve. Please, Aaron." She leaned down and claimed his mouth and his heart.

CHAPTER 10

One thing was for sure – she may be innocent, but she knew how to drive him mad. Her legs were tucked on either side of him and her center was pressed up against him. Her mouth was roaming over his face and neck, placing light kisses where she could and setting him on fire. She was driving him crazy and unless he slowed her down, her first time would be here on the couch and over before either of them knew it.

Grabbing her hips, he hoisted her up into his arms. She wrapped her legs around his waist, latching onto him, while continuing to nibble on his ear. When he started walking she let out a quick breath against his neck and held on as he walked towards the bedroom.

Laying her down gently on the bed, he stood over her, with her short hair in tuffs and her lips swollen.

She was aching for him to kiss her again. She reached up to push her hair from her face so she could see him. She was nervous when she smiled up at him, but held her hands up, inviting him down onto the bed with her.

He went into her arms and started to kiss her again. He

paused, pushed her hands over her head, and looked down into her eyes. They were the color of the sky after a good storm; he felt as if he was a drowning man. He couldn't get enough air or enough of her; he could see her eyes cloud over when he ran his hand up her side lightly.

She moved her hips and wrapped her legs around his, trying to pull him closer.

"Aaron, please." It was barely a whisper.

"Let me take care of you," he said as their lips met again.

He heard her moan as he reached down and started unbuttoning her blouse. Tiny goose bumps spread across her skin as his fingertips touched her.

What was he doing? He was going to torture her with his gentleness. One moment she felt like she was melting and the next like she was going to explode if he didn't hurry up.

He pulled her shirt gently off her shoulders. Placing his mouth at the base of her neck, he saw her milky white shoulders. They felt so soft that he wanted to spend hours exploring the spot. She tasted like heaven and he couldn't get enough. As he ran his hands over her small breasts and stomach, he noticed that she wore a deep green bra with red lady bugs on the straps, and he smiled. He could go nuts for a woman with an eccentric taste in undergarments.

He pulled the straps down over her shoulders. She moaned quietly as he pulled them lower still. Her breath quickened, and her heart fluttered with a slight touch of his mouth. She was small and firm but very sensitive. As he reached around and undid the straps, he released her to his view and let out a small moan himself.

"Beautiful," he mumbled against her skin.

"Please, please," Lacey said over and over, feeling like she was on fire just for his touch.

"Yes? What is it, Lacey?" He smiled down at her. He ran

his fingertips over her heated skin and started tracing kisses across her stomach.

Her hips jerked every time he would get near her stomach.

"I need you." She walked her hands up under his shirt and pulled it over his head.

He was exquisite. She could see his shoulders were wide, and he was covered with tan skin. He sat still as she explored his body with her eyes. There was a light trail of dusty colored hair that went from his belly button down to below his pants making her want to explore beyond, so she ran her hands over him. She could tell he spent time working out as well as working on the house. She wanted to explore more of him. Running her hands over his stomach, she felt his muscles bunch under her fingers

He let her explore his chest and stomach as he had done to her; it was pure torture. She had a determined look on her face, so he sat back and did not interfere. But when she gripped his jeans at the buttons, he pulled her hands aside. Again, he chuckled at the sound she made, along with the frustrated look she gave him.

Taking her hands in one of his, he pinned them down again and ran his hand up her torso, stopping briefly to undo her black work slacks. He slid them over and down her narrow hips.

How could someone so small have such long legs? he thought as he ran his hands over her. She moved under him, meeting his hands by flexing her back and arching towards him.

Leaning over her, he claimed her mouth once more and rolled with her across the soft bed.

Her hands, once freed, rushed to pull his jeans down over his hips. She was burning and felt she needed speed, but every time she tried urging him, he pulled back and slowed down his movements. He was driving her crazy.

When they finally had all barriers removed, both were panting. He tilted his head back and looked at her; he thought she was a goddess. He had never seen anything so perfect as the creature lying below him. Her eyes sparkled, and a smile formed at the corner of her lips, causing something inside him to crack. He tried to pull back, but she wrapped herself around him, pulling him closer.

She thought she could see fear creep into his eyes, but there was no going back now, so she held on tight and promised herself to think later.

"You're not getting out of this that easy," she said against his chest. She could feel the apprehension leaving his body. His hands came up; his fingers spread in her hair, pulling her mouth back to his. She felt him tremble when she ran her hands lightly down his stomach, and he sucked in his breath when she wrapped her hand around his length.

He was trying, really trying to go slow. But she was doing such a good job of driving him crazy. He just could not stop himself from pushing harder and faster. Pushing her back, he quickly sheathed himself.

"Hang on to me, baby," he said, and gently slid into her. There was a quick flash of pain, but then there was nothing but pleasure as he moved slowly inside her. He gripped her right hand, holding it above her head with their fingers intertwined. His mouth moved to hers, trying to set a slow pace, gently torturing them both. She felt their need building as the speed of their loving gained.

He tried again to slow the pace, to keep them both in the moment, but they were both slipping in and out of control of their bodies.

When she threw back her head with her eyes closed, and he felt her convulse around him, he lost control. He grabbed her hips and took her higher for a second time. He rolled them both over, so she was straddling him, and when he felt her need building again, he held tighter to her hips to guide her to their completion.

Lacey matched Aaron's steady slow heart beat, letting her rhythm slow to match his. The left side of her cheek was being tickled by the cover of light hair on Aaron's chest. She smiled and stretched into him as he rubbed his hands gently up her back.

She had known it would be like this; she'd always imagined love would be just like this. She had never been one to deny her feelings. This left her open to teasing from her brothers, but she hadn't cared. Here was the man she'd been waiting for, and she was going to enjoy every minute of pleasure with him, holding on to the hope that it would last.

He removed his hands from her back and she let out a little pout, causing him to chuckle.

"More?" he said against her forehead.

"Mmm," she tried to reply, but was so relaxed all she could manage was a moan.

She let out a quick gasp as she was swiftly flipped over onto her stomach. Aaron's legs were pinning her hips down as he straddled her. Letting out another laugh, he began to massage her lower back.

"You know, you really should take better care of yourself," he said, working his way up to her shoulders. He could feel the tension in the muscles of her back, tight with knots.

"Yes, Doctor." She smiled into the comforter when he gave her bottom a quick slap.

"I like your birthmark," he said, tracing the small tan mark on her lower back. It reminded him of Australia, which only caused him to smile even more.

"Mmm," she moaned again as he continued his exploration of her back. He moved lower to her legs. When he got down to her feet he noticed the small blister on her foot.

"You're on your feet too much," he frowned. "Why don't you take a day off now and then?" He said.

"I usually don't work this hard," she said and stretched her arms above her head.

"Only when you're trying to avoid me?" He turned her over and began on her front. He noticed that she seemed to have no modesty.

"I wasn't avoiding you," she said, looking up into his eyes. But her look gave her away.

"Oh, really?" He ran a hand down her body. "Then what would you call it? Face it, Lacey, you've been avoiding me. Why?"

"You think a lot of yourself, don't you, doctor," she countered and started to sit up.

"Don't," he said, and she relaxed back onto the bed.

"Maybe I've been doing some avoiding of my own," he said sleepily, lying down beside her. He pulled her close so that her head rested on his shoulder.

"Why?" she asked in a whisper.

"You do things to me, that I don't know what to think of yet." Pulling her closer, he kissed the top of her head. "I've just come out of a bad relationship and wasn't looking for anything, yet."

She waited until his breathing slowed, steadied. "I'm sorry I avoided you," she said, nuzzling into his chest.

"Good." He let out a soft yawn and promptly fell asleep. Lacey stayed awake to listen to his heart beat against her cheek and fell asleep thinking about the man who was quietly snoring next to her.

WHEN SHE FELT light fingers run up her ribs, she inhaled and tried not to squirm. Only her brothers knew her ribs were ticklish. These fingers didn't mean to tickle her but arouse her as they ran down her ribs and hips to the outside of her thighs. They lightly traced the muscles of her legs, then circled toward the inside of her legs. Slowly they moved up higher, pulsing toward her, and closing in on her. When he lightly touched her with a whisper, she let out a low moan.

She sure was hard to wake up, but Aaron was enjoying seeing how much he could get away with and for how long before her eyes finally fluttered open. Several times she had sighed and moaned when he had run his fingers over her delicate skin. Once she'd sucked in her breath after his fingers had run over a particular rib. He would have to explore that ticklish spot later. Now he wanted to make her want him as much as he was aching for her. After having woken up with her soft body wrapped around his, the soft scent of her lying next to him, he was full of purpose.

He became even more aroused when he found her moist for him. Spreading her legs gently, he started to explore her as she let out another moan and turned her head to the side. He eased back, and she settled back down.

When he finally entered her, it was with slow and easy movements. Her eyes opened, and she grabbed his shoulders.

She came awake quickly now, and when she opened her eyes, Aaron filled her vision. He was smiling down at her as he moved.

"Good morning." He leaned down and kissed her until she was out of breath.

When she surfaced again, it was to the soft sound of rain. The empty spot next to her was still warm, so she looked around. She saw the blinds had been closed only allowing minimal light in. Rolling over, she gasped at the alarm clock, and jumped out of bed and began searching for her clothes which were nowhere in sight. Quickly yanking open the dresser drawers, she settled for one of Aaron's white tee shirts and some gray sweats that she had to roll up four times to see her feet.

She started out of the bedroom and paused when she heard Aaron on the phone. She headed towards his voice and reached the room just as he slammed down his phone in disgust.

"Is there a problem?" Lacey walked up behind him and reached for him.

"It's nothing." He pulled away from her and started to pace in front of the empty fireplace.

Lacey watched him pace and saw his frustration build.

She walked over, took his hand and said, "How about I make us some breakfast?"

If he wasn't ready to open up, she would just have to break down his barriers little by little.

Aaron sat at his counter watching her quick and steady movements while she prepared breakfast. He enjoyed watching her and noticed that she looked more relaxed this morning. The circles under her eyes were gone and she was humming to herself. He could just imagine her dressed like this and doing the same things in this kitchen for years to come.

Not wanting the moment to end, he thought of his plans. He knew he wasn't due at the office until later that day; his first appointment was at eleven, but he would have gladly blown everyone off to be able to spend the whole day with her in his house.

"What are you doing for Thanksgiving?" Lacey looked up from her task of moving the cooked eggs to plates.

"I suppose I'll be spending it with my Grandfather. I hadn't really thought about it yet."

"What about your folks?" she asked, setting a full plate in front of him, then taking her own next to him.

"Well, I haven't heard from them in maybe eight months. They are somewhere in Europe, I think."

"Won't they be coming home for the holidays?" She took a piece of bacon and nibbled it.

He thought of that word, 'home,' and almost laughed. "My folks and I came to an arrangement years ago, about the holidays. They spend them somewhere tropical and ignore the fact that they have a son, and I spend my time doing whatever I want to do without them. It's for the best, really." His voice held no bitterness, he believed every word.

"That is their loss. Would you like to spend it with us? I can promise you good food, good company, cold beer, and football on the big screen," she smiled. She couldn't understand a family who wouldn't want to be together during the holidays but knowing this little fact from his past made her want to get her hands on his parents.

THE FOOTBALL GAME WAS EXCITING, the beer was cold, and the food was excellent. But according to Aaron, the best part of the day was the company. Everyone was together and having a good time. Aaron's stomach was full and he had a cold beer in his hand. He felt, maybe for the first time in his life, like he was part a family.

His grandfather was there, sitting in a big recliner; his eyes were glued to the TV set. Occasionally he would stand to scream at the set, along with the rest of the group.

Megan and Todd sat on the love seat in front of the windows. Megan had a blanket wrapped around her with her feet in her husband's lap. Todd occasionally rubbed them for her, but he was more into the game at the moment than rubbing his pregnant wife's feet.

Iian had poured his tall frame into the other recliner in the room, while Aaron and Lacey sat next to him on the other couch. She had on a bright green Oregon Ducks sweatshirt with matching socks; her feet were tucked up underneath her.

The brothers bantered, joked, taunted, and laughed with each other throughout the game. This was something Aaron had never seen in his entire life. At first he was uncomfortable, thinking they were mad at each other, but soon he learned this was a normal pastime between the family members. Lacey always appeared to be in the middle of each argument, egging her brothers along and never really taking sides.

Aaron wondered how a woman who was half the size of her brothers held such power over the two men. When she asked for more chips, Iian had not even blinked at the request and had slipped out of the room to fill another bowl. Todd had tried to put his feet on the coffee table at one point; it had only taken a single look from Lacey to get his feet back firmly on the ground. To be this close as siblings amazed Aaron, and at the same time, he had never been more jealous in his life.

All this thinking about families drew out old memories of his childhood. He must have been around the age of eight when he presented to his parents a chart he had drawn up, outlining a list of reasons why he should have a brother. In his eight-year-old mind, a brother could play with him; he wouldn't be so lonely. He could guide and protect his younger sibling, and maybe he would have someone who would love him unconditionally.

Shaking his head, he recalled his parent's response to his request. He recalled also the new boarding school he had then been sent to. It was stricter than the prior schools; they frowned upon and tried to discourage such behavior in children...

LACEY HAD NOTICED the minute Aaron stopped focusing on the game. When he withdrew into his own world his face changed, his shoulders tightened, and he gripped his knees with his hands. The major clue to his introspection, however, was that the last touchdown had been celebrated by every man in the room, except one. Then as quickly as his mood had come on, it was gone with a shake of his head, and he seemed to rejoin the group for the rest of the game.

She wondered what it would take to break down the barriers he held so tightly around his thoughts.

She really enjoyed watching him interact with her family. She also thought everyone had gotten along wonderfully, especially after Aaron had relaxed. However, by the time everyone was ready to leave for the evening, she began to worry that she had trusted him with the most precious gift of her heart while he had yet to open up his own heart to her. Something, she thought, that should have come along with the intimacy they had shared. Maybe he just needed more time. Megan had needed time to accept love when she had first arrived in Pride. Maybe Aaron needed the same thing—time.

AARON GOT home after dropping off his grandfather and was headed back to the kitchen for one more beer when he saw the message light blinking on his machine. Pausing in the entryway, he shrugged out of his coat and hit the button as he continued into the kitchen. When he heard his mother's voice, his hand stopped on its way to the refrigerator door. His mind froze and after a second, he could feel his heart rate increase. He heard a buzzing in his ears and shook his head to clear it. Rushing back to the machine, he hit the rewind button.

"Aaron. We are shocked to hear that you're in Oregon and don't know what you're doing there. We've talked to Jennifer and think it's time you resolved your problem and stopped running away from your commitments. Your father and I expect this embarrassing situation to be handled before the wedding. We expect to see you in California when we get there after the New Year."

No "hello", no "goodbye", no "how are you?" Nothing personal—that was his parents.

Storming to the fridge, he yanked it open and grabbed a beer. He needed it now, along with a few others.

CHAPTER 11

*T*he days after a holiday were always busy. It was strange how people flocked to homemade food one day and then the next they wanted someone else to do the cooking for them. Maybe it was the dishes they didn't want to deal with, or maybe it was just getting away from their homes. Whatever it was, Lacey enjoyed these busy times. The sounds and smells of it all felt like home to her.

She knew that people were out making their black Friday purchases, pushing and shoving each other at the closest malls. She, on the other hand, had nothing to worry about because she had most of her Christmas shopping done early, thanks to her favorite online stores.

It was half way through the dinner rush when she felt that familiar tingle down her spine. Looking over, she saw Aaron walk in and take a seat at the bar located along the far wall. Mary, the bartender on duty, quickly rushed over to take his order.

After dropping off her latest order, she took a minute to stop at the bar.

"Did you want some dinner?" she said, kissing him

quickly. She sat next to him and tried not to notice how he had stiffened a little at her light touch.

"No, just a quick drink, that is all I want right now." He nodded his thanks as Mary set down a whiskey. "Since this is the only bar that's open right now…" he trailed off and drank the whiskey in a single swallow.

"Oh, okay," she said, and noticed she was being hailed by the couple at table twelve. "I'll be right back." She rushed back to work.

Twenty minutes later she stopped back at the bar. She didn't know how many drinks he'd had, but by his look, she was sure the bar stool wouldn't hold him up much longer.

"Want that dinner now?" she asked him. Her shift was almost over, and the majority of people had cleared out, leaving the restaurant almost empty.

Mary delivered another drink to Aaron, shook her head at Lacey, then went to the end of the bar and started clearing some dishes, leaving them alone again.

"Are you alright? Has something happened?" she placed her hand on his forearm, noticing his eyes were red and blood shot.

He laughed quickly, "My life." He shook his head after downing the whiskey. "My parents." Wishing for another shot, he started to wave to the bartender.

Lacey quickly grabbed his arm. "How about I take you home. You can tell me about it."

Looking into her eyes, he saw concern and something more—he saw trust.

"I just can't deal with this." He shook his head and started to get up. She grabbed his arm and shaking her head, she looked into his eyes.

He could only guess at what she saw there. Hell, he'd gotten drunk two nights in a row, not just a little drunk, but rip-roaring drunk. He had woken with the taste of cotton in his mouth and his head felt as if someone had split it in two with an ax.

He had thought about his messed-up childhood and his potential marriage disaster. Now, according to his parents, he was the one screwing this up. It appeared they expected him to make it *"right"* before the wedding. Just what the hell did they mean by that?

"Aaron." Hearing his name shook him free of this thought and he looked into her face. "Let me take you home."

"I'm fine," he said, and started to walk away. He would walk home, maybe that would clear his head. He doubted it, but it was worth a try.

"If you don't want me to stick around, I won't." She took his arm again to steady him. "But I'm still driving you home. It's going to snow later."

As they walked by the end of the bar, Lacey informed Mary that she was dropping Aaron off at home. "Tell Katie to take over my tables, will you?"

"Sure, I'll let her know. Goodnight." Mary gave Lacey a quick smile.

When the cold night air hit him, he seemed to break through the haze his mind had been in since he received the phone message.

"My truck's over there," he said, handing her his keys.

He remained silent during the short drive to his place. His mother's voice was playing around in his head, as they passed the pine tree in the middle of town square. The tree was decorated with all different colored lights and ornaments. He noticed that each of the street lights had ornamental decorations hanging from them. Each house they passed had lights or decorations; it seemed the whole town was lit up.

Seeing his own newly installed driveway lights did little to lift his spirits. He had wanted to see Lacey, but when he sat at the bar, the only thing he could think about was the phone message, and self-pity had taken over. What was he doing here? Did he really think he could hide from his parents? Did he really want to? Did he really think he could start fresh?

Man, he wanted another beer. Drowning his problems had worked for him last night. Sure he had woken up on the floor in his living room with a splitting headache, but he was sure he had spent most of the night on the soft leather couch. Maybe he should have stayed home tonight.

STOPPING JUST in front of the newly installed garage doors, Lacey turned off the truck and turned to face him. She could hear the light drizzle of rain hitting the roof of the truck. They sat there for a while looking at each other.

"Please tell me this isn't to do with us?"

He quickly turned his head towards her.

"No," he said, and turned back to look at his house. "It's funny, you know, you wouldn't think I would put so much stock in something like a house." He sat and looked at the place. She turned and did the same.

"It's a nice place. It doesn't even look like the same house." She turned to him. "You should be very proud of it and yourself."

When he let out a breath, she asked, "Are you going to tell me what this is all about?"

"Let's go inside, I'll get a fire going." He got out and made it halfway around the truck before she started to follow him.

As he bent over the paper and wood in the family room fireplace, she walked into the kitchen and started a pot of coffee.

After the coffee was done, she took two mugs into the

room. She saw him sitting on the couch staring into the flames. For the first time since meeting him, he looked lonely and lost.

"I thought I could break away from them." He took the mug from her and set the cup on the coffee table without taking a sip. She shook her head and sitting next to him, handed the cup to him again. This time she made sure he took a drink. "I don't drink like that, often," he sat the cup down again. "I just wanted you to know."

"I think I'm a good judge of character, Aaron. I don't see 'alcoholic' written anywhere on you. Please, just talk to me. Tell me what set this off." She reached for his hands and held them.

He laughed. "What else—my parents."

"And?" She tucked her legs under her. She could hear the rain start up again outside and grabbed her mug to warm her cold hands.

"Apparently, they just found out that I moved here, and they are not pleased. They expect me to be back in L.A. by New Year's." He set the coffee down again and looked into the fire as if to find a solution there. "All my life I have done what they expected of me, thinking," he shook his head, "no, hoping, that by obeying them, I would change them. Change the way they felt about me."

He leaned back and stared at the ceiling.

"It was always like this. I went to the schools they wanted. I took the jobs they wanted. I remember before I graduated, sending out my internship requests. I wanted to intern in New York, they wanted me to intern in Boston. More money, more power. To them I was a pawn they could move around to better their lives."

He closed his eyes and rubbed his forehead.

"So, I interned in Boston; afterword's, they wanted me to take a job in Philadelphia. Taking the job in Los Angeles was the first thing I had ever done against their wishes. Now they are upset at me for leaving the job in L.A." A short burst of laughter escaped, and he shook his head.

"I'm tired of trying to please them. Taking over for my grandfather was the first thing that I have done right. This house feels right—it is right—being here." He stopped and looked at her. Words could not express what he felt, or how he felt.

"Aaron, from the sound of it, your parents aren't very, well…," she didn't quite know what to say, "…good parents. I'm so sorry they hurt you." Setting her own coffee down next to his, she took his hands again.

"I can't imagine the childhood you had being an only child and living alone in boarding schools. I have always had brothers who helped me through rough times like when we lost our father. They were always there for me growing up, but I can't imagine what it would be like without the love and the support of a family. I do know that your grandfather loves you though. Further, you are here now, in this place, with us, and you have friends and a home. Blood makes them your parents, but that doesn't make their opinion of you important. You can make your own choices now. You have to make a life for yourself, one that you can live with." Taking his face in her hands, she pulled him in for a soft kiss.

"I'm sorry that they've caused you pain, but that's all over now. You're here, with me." She kissed his lips again.

He found her lips like a drug, soft and smooth. Running his hands up her arms, he could feel her shiver at his touch. Her hands were in his hair, pulling him in closer. She hadn't come here for this. This was the first time he'd opened up to her. How could she not come to his aid?

Her skin was so soft, and she tasted so good that he left hot trails down her neck. Stopping frequently to sample, he pulled her shirt over her head. He was nibbling his way along her shoulder when he saw that her bright yellow lace bra had little white flowers covering the straps.

"How is it your undergarments always make me smile," he said, slowly pulling down the flowered strap. Her head dropped back, and a soft moan escaped her lips.

Reaching around her back, he released the clasp and filled his hands with her. When she straddled him, he leaned back and enjoyed the feel of her legs tightly wrapped around his hips. The hem of her black work skirt was hiked up past her thighs, and he ran his hands up her thighs and pushed it up even further. She wore black tights and after some maneuvering, he finally pulled them down and off her legs, leaving them bare and allowing her to straddle him again.

Letting his hands roam free, he glanced down and noticed her undergarments were a matching set. Giving one more smile, he pulled the lace to the side. He purred when he found her moist and ready for him.

"Now, Aaron, now. Please." She reached for him, helping him free himself from the confines of his jeans. In one swift motion he grabbed her hips and was inside her.

How could she have ever known that it would be like this? She could feel her heartbeat racing to match their rhythm. She could see matching desire in his eyes and, she hoped, love. He increased the speed and her head fell back, giving him access to her neck once again.

"Ride me, Lacey. God, please ride me," he said into her neck, breathing harder than he ever had in his life.

Moving her hips to an internal beat, she started slowly, torturing herself and him. His hands gripped her hips, holding her. She began to speed up. How could she have ever known that sex would be like this: this closeness—this wanting. It tied her up and built something heavy in her chest. Looking down into his face, she saw that his eyes were on her. She could see the matching desire there. He reached up and took her nipple between his fingers lightly. Her head fell back, and her speed increased.

"Please." It was more a gasp than a plea.

"Take all of me, Lacey." He grabbed her hips and took them faster until release came. It was swifter and more powerful than anything he had ever felt before. She relaxed against his chest as he pulled her closer and breathed in her scent.

It must have been only a few minutes, but when his head settled back onto his shoulders, he realized his stomach was making the growling sounds, and he laughed.

"I guess a whole day of drinking and no food does something to a man," he said, laughing. She pulled back and looked at him.

"Are you telling me you've been drinking all day and haven't eaten anything? And you call yourself a doctor?" She got up, and grabbing her clothes, made a sprint for the bathroom.

Five minutes later she walked into his kitchen. He had pulled on his jeans but not a shirt. His bare feet and *"just had sex"* hair gave him a dangerous look. He was bent over searching his refrigerator, which made his low riding jeans show off his perfect backside. She leaned against the door and admired the view.

"Well, I have left over pizza, some old sandwich meat, or we can make some eggs," he said, turning his head towards her.

"I have a better idea." she said as she walked slowly towards him, smiling.

An hour and some cold pizza later, she jumped up and quickly dressed again. Then she walked over to the closet and put on her coat while holding out his. "Come on. I have another idea," she said, smiling at him.

Her first *idea* had been a great one, and he was enjoying

the after effects of two really great bouts of sex, so he figured he would go along with whatever her new plans might be. Pulling on his clothes, he walked over to take the coat from her.

When she opened the back door, Bernard was sitting there in fresh snow, tail wagging and tongue drooling. He had a ball in his mouth. The dog had a keen sense of where she was and tended to follow her.

"Good, we are all here." She reached down and gave the ball a good toss. Turning back to Aaron, she said, "Hang on a minute." She raced out the back door and within a minute, she was back with a huge ax.

"Listen honey, that thing is sharp," he said, backing away with his hands drawn up in surrender.

She laughed, "Oh, please. This isn't for you. It's for the tree." She pulled him out the back door and looked up at the snowflakes.

"See, I told you. Snow! This is going to be perfect," she said, leading the way down the path into the woods.

"Tree, what tree?" he asked, following her and shoving his cold hands into his coat pockets where he was happy to discover a pair of gloves. Putting them on quickly, he caught up with Lacey and the dog.

"A Christmas tree, of course. It's a family tradition to chop down one after Thanksgiving," she stated as she reached in her other pocket and pulled out a knitted hat with yellow daisies that matched her gloves. He smiled as he thought they also matched her panties and bra.

They walked through the woods with Bernard trailing behind, an ax flung over Aaron's shoulder as the snowflakes got bigger. The flakes were wet and somehow found their way down between the tall trees to land softly on his exposed neck. Pulling his collar tighter, he noticed how the forest was so quiet while it was snowing. He could hear their feet hitting the path, the dog panting, and he swore he could hear the falling snow softly hit the branches of the trees themselves.

"The Christmas tree tradition was part of every holiday season. We've been doing it since before I was born," she said, smiling at him. She continued to walk down the path as Bernard trailed behind like it was the most natural thing to be walking in the dark woods in the snow.

Wanting to tease her a little, he said, "You know I have a plastic tree in a box out in the garage. I was just going to put it up sometime next week."

"Plastic!" She stopped dead in the middle of the pathway and faced him. "Plastic! There will be no plastic trees in your new house. Do you understand me, Doctor Stevens?" She shook her head and continued down the path.

"We always get the best Christmas trees from up on Temple Ridge, but it's late and cold tonight. I don't feel like hiking two miles up and back again. Thank goodness you have me along tonight because I know of the perfect tree. I spotted it earlier this year and have had it in mind ever since."

They rounded a corner in the path and she headed off into the trees with Bernard following. After a shake of his head, he headed in after her.

THE TREE BRANCHES were thick and the snow seemed to have a harder time finding its way down to the ground. The temperature warmed a little and the smell of pine filled the air. He could see the branches of the trees swaying in the wind as the snow continued to fall. Snowflakes stuck to his lashes and tickled his nose. Had he ever walked in the woods with a girl, an ax, and a dog?

Looking back to where Lacey had been, he froze. She had disappeared again.

Glancing around, he wondered how such a small thing could move so fast. Of course, it didn't help that he was still half hammered. He called to her as he turned around in circles.

Nothing. The quiet night seemed to engulf him again. Finally, she emerged on his left, smiling.

"Over here. I've found it!" She turned and walked back into the darkness. This time he followed and kept closer to her than before.

He felt that she belonged here amongst the trees and snow, like a fairy-tale creature. He had thought that description fit her since he had first seen her.

Reaching the edge of a clearing, she turned to stand beside a rather large pine tree. At least he thought it was a pine. It smelled like the pine soap he used to wash up with after painting. It had perfect branches and not a needle was out of place. It was roughly seven feet tall and the best-looking Christmas tree he'd ever seen. He agreed that it was just what the house needed.

She smiled at him and placed one hand on her hip. "Are you ready to chop down our first tree?"

He looked at her and thought she was just like the tree—exactly what he needed.

CHAPTER 12

*I*f she had thought about it, she would have realized she was settling into a pattern. Lacey worked her shifts at the restaurant, and in the evenings would end up at Aaron's place.

It had taken them a full night to decorate the tree and the rest of the house with ornaments from a box in his garage. She even brought some of her own lights and holiday knick-knacks over. They played Christmas music and laughed and sang along the entire time it took them to decorate. The house looked festive and was really starting to feel like a home.

Aaron would work away on the place every night, painting and hammering and working out little details that made it feel finished. She enjoyed helping or sometimes just ended up watching him work.

Bernard had learned to sit on Aaron's back porch every afternoon waiting for Lacey to arrive. Aaron had even bought him a dog bed. It had started out in his laundry room, but Bernard kept dragging it into the living room right in front of the fireplace. Aaron, being the softy that he was, had let it remain there.

For once in her life, Lacey was in a relationship that she didn't feel completely in control of. She didn't know how to feel about it, but she planned to enjoy it while it lasted.

On nights she worked the early shift, she would bring dinner or would cook at Aaron's. The house would be filled with the smells of home cooking, and laughter always sounded out as they shared these meals. She really did enjoy her time with him, but she enjoyed the nights spent in his arms even better.

———

THE NIGHT of the school Christmas play had been creeping up. She had promised her friend Becca Linden, a grade school teacher, that she would assist with the backdrops. She dragged Aaron along to help with the designs. Because organizational and artistic talent had run in her family for generations, everyone in town always called on a Jordan to help out.

The school play this year was the classic A Christmas Carol and was less than a week away. Lacey was in charge of drawing and painting three backdrops that included, a bedroom, a snowy hilltop cemetery, and the inside of a small house, complete with a fireplace.

Lacey had outlined all three backdrops while Aaron chatted comfortably with several kids who were eagerly waiting to help paint.

She liked that he looked relaxed around the small kids. Of course, it helped that most of them had visited his offices and actually knew him. He was a lot like his grandfather when it came to interacting with his patients.

She could tell that most of the kids looked up to him.

They would tug on his shirt until he gave them his full attention. He would always bend down and look them directly in the eyes when he spoke to them.

Smiling, she turned to the excited group. "I'm done." When every eye turned in her direction there was a choir of "ooh, aah and wow."

"I've marked what each section should be colored, so it should be easy." She showed them the little color marks. "Everyone can grab a brush and some paint. Remember, try to stay in the lines and no eating the paint." She said this just as a William, a small but sinister little boy, held out a brush full of midnight blue to Reagan. William, Lacey knew, always dared Reagan to do things. And of course, Reagan always took to the bait.

Two hours and a huge headache later, Lacey and Aaron sat in the front row of the auditorium alone and looked at the final product. The kids rushed off with the promise of milk and cookies, most of them covered with paint, all of them with smiles on their faces.

The backdrops stood hanging on stands so the paint would dry. Up close, they appeared to be painted by a bunch of fourth graders. Well, they had been painted by a bunch of fourth graders. But when Aaron and Lacey looked at them from seats in the front row, they looked better. A little better, at least.

OVER THE NEXT FEW WEEKS, Lacey found herself even busier than normal. With Christmas just around the corner, she found it harder and harder to divide her time between the restaurant, her house, swim lessons, and Aaron's place.

This week in particular was a very busy week because she was attempting to help her very good friend Allison close her family business, Adams Antiques. Lacey had babysat Allison and her sister, Abby, when they were younger. Abby had died years ago from Leukemia, just after their father had died, leaving Allison and her mother alone. Allison had then taken over her family's business at a young age.

Now Allison was moving to Los Angeles to start her art career, a career that Megan had helped kick off by taking some of Allison's art to Ric Derby, a friend who owned The Blue Spot, a chain of art galleries.

Currently, Lacey and Megan were helping Allison pack up some remaining items in the store for shipment to California.

"I can't thank you enough for coming and helping me out. I never dreamed I would be leaving Pride to pursue my dreams." Allison sat in the middle of the shop floor with boxes and tissue paper surrounding her. "Did you know that Ric called me this morning and said that he sold twelve of my pieces? Twelve!" She stared at her two friends. All three of the women were sitting around the middle of the floor packing various trinkets and knickknacks into the boxes.

Megan was currently in the last trimester of her pregnancy and sat happily on a cushion with her feet tucked under her.

"I knew it! The minute I saw your art I just knew it would be a big hit." Megan smiled. "I just wish you were staying in town a little longer, at least until I give birth." She rubbed her growing stomach.

"Me, too, but I'll be back this summer to visit. It's only a day's drive up and it's not like I'm moving across the country like you did." She looked around the almost empty room and sighed.

"But it's still scary. I've never lived anywhere but here." This had been her whole life. She could still close her eyes and see herself sitting in the corner at a small antique table playing tea with Abby. Or look across the room and see her father and mother kissing behind the old wood counter top.

"I guess it helped closing shop the week before Christmas." Looking around the room again, she noticed how empty it was and her eyes started to mist. "There are only these boxes and some other furniture in the back room now. Everything else sold on Black Friday."

"The antique baby crib and changing table I bought from you last week go perfectly in the baby's room. Todd just loved the cherry wood. He is going to look at getting me a rocking chair to match," Megan said, reaching over and patting Allison's arm.

"Speaking of the baby, do you know if you are having a boy or a girl?" Allison asked as she taped up the last box.

"We could have found out a while back, but we want to be surprised."

"I know what you're having," Lacey said, smiling. "But I'm keeping it a secret, too."

"You think you know what I'm having." Megan laughed. She stopped laughing and looked at Lacey. "However, with your track record I may not want to hear your theory."

They all laughed.

"I'm going to miss this," Allison said, taking a breath. "Am I doing the right thing moving to California? Please tell me I'm not crazy."

"When I decided to travel for a year after graduation, I thought the same thing. I'm here to tell you my eyes were opened during that year of traveling. It gave me something you just can't experience here in Pride. And you can always come back home. Will you be coming home again?" The two friends sat quietly waiting for her answer.

"I can't imagine myself anywhere else. I'm going to California for experience and to help my art career. I want to define it better, fine tune it some, and then try to figure out whatever else Mr. Derby has in store for me." She wiped away a tear.

"Then let's have a toast." Lacey said, holding up her juice cup and waiting for her friends to do the same. "A toast to best friends, travel, and experiencing life. But most importantly, a toast to returning to Pride."

He had a bottle of champagne cooling next to the wine glasses and candles on the coffee table. The smoked salmon was warming in the oven along with the green beans surrounded by sweet potatoes. Everything was in place. Turning on the radio, he hunted until he found something soft and smokey for background music. The fire crackled as he walked over and dimmed the overhead lights. Perfection.

Bernard snored on his doggie bed, which Aaron had pushed to the corner of the living room. The dog was beginning to think he lived here. Every time Aaron drove up his drive, he was sitting at the front door waiting for him usually with a ball or a stick in his mouth. He had to admit, it felt pretty good to have him there, always waiting.

Tonight, however, it wasn't the company of the dog, but the dog's owner, he was looking for. And it appeared she was running late.

Taking his cell out of his slacks he texted the man who would know where she was.

"Where is your sister? --Aaron"

A few moments later he checked the reply.

"She left work five minutes ago. Should be heading your way now—later, Iian."

Just as he read the last of the message, he heard her car drive up. Smiling to himself, he heard Bernard groan and glanced over as the dog stood from his bed and rushed over to the front door.

"Yeah, buddy, she's home." He opened the door just as Lacey reached for the handle. She had a bundle of white flowers in one hand and a wrapped box in the other.

"Hello," he said, just looking at her. She wore her long green winter coat; the hood was up because it had been lightly snowing. Helping her out of the coat, he shook the snow off before placing it along his in the front closet.

Bernard let out a quick happy bark. Setting the flowers and box down, she bent to pat him.

"Welcome to my finished home," he said as she stood back up. He circled her in his arms and kissed her softly, slowly.

He noticed she had changed out of her work clothes and was wearing a silver dress that clung to her curves. The dress had long sleeves, but he had felt that her back had been left exposed. As he pulled back to look at her, he noticed that the front dipped down in a gentle slope. The way the dress accented the curve of her back and her perfect breasts distracted him from the gifts she had brought.

She enjoyed the sexy looks he was giving her. She picked up the flowers and box once more.

"Finished?" she asked. "A home isn't complete until you receive your first house warming present." She handed him the flowers and box. "Let's go sit by the fire so you can open your gift." With her free hands she pulled him towards the couch.

He chuckled as he sat next to her. He was glad he had planned a celebration dinner to mark the finishing of the renovations on his house. They had hung the last door along with the bedroom window blinds last night; the place was done.

Taking one last glance at her, he started opening the wrapping on the box. She noticed that he was the type of person who unwrapped slowly, pulling each corner back and unfolding the wrapping like it was made of gold instead of paper.

"Oh no, you're one of *those* people," she said. Her fingers itched to rip at the paper that she had carefully wrapped earlier that day.

"I am a doctor, we like to be precise." He smiled at her. "I suppose you like to rip the paper, and no doubt, shake all the boxes beforehand."

"Of course." She held her breath when he opened the box.

The vase was crystal with blue flowers, it wasn't new, it wasn't perfect, but it was beautiful.

"It's beautiful," he said, holding it up so the light from the fire shone through it.

"It was one of my mother's. She always had flowers in the house no matter what time of year." She grabbed the bundle he had set down on the table. He set the vase down on the coffee table so she could place the flowers in it. "She always said flowers in a house helped make it home."

Smiling at her, he took her face in his hands. "It's perfect, thank you," he said as he laid a soft kiss on her lips.

"Welcome home, Aaron," she said, then kissed him.

Later that evening, as the weather was turning colder, and the light rain was beginning to look more like snow, his grandfather stopped by and quickly dropped off his house warming present. The old brass key hanger which had always hung in his grandfather's office now hung just inside Aaron's back door. Another perfect present.

Todd and Megan stopped by the next day and delivered a front door brass knocker with Aaron's name inscribed on it. And Iian had walked over in the rain to deliver a pan of fresh sticky buns along with a set of kitchen cutlery. Aaron had been informed that no kitchen was complete without the proper knives.

There had been others stopping by throughout the week, all bringing small gifts that included food. He welcomed them all and was an expert at showing off his remodeled home by the time the snow started falling again later that week. With all the company, Lacey had come up with a brilliant plan to have a house warming party on New Year's Eve.

Planning a party was something Aaron had never done before. Lacey helped of course, but she left a lot of the major decisions up to him.

One evening he had been over at his grandfather's house getting a list of people to invite. His grandfather had, after all, lived in town all of his eighty-seven years. He knew everyone to invite. Aaron liked the old man's place. It always reminded him of a hunting lodge. It was a large wood cabin with oversized windows that faced a small creek. It was built in the same place his great-grandparents house had been.

His grandfather had spent his youth here, only going away to serve in the Army for three years. He always recounted that he had come home a changed man. Gone was the desire to travel and see far off places. Landing in Poland at the end of World War II had taken that desire away and replaced it with one to help and protect the people of his small town.

Aaron had always loved to sit and listen to his grandfather's stories when he visited as a child. There were times he had wished he could have stayed with him on a permanent basis.

Now he and Lacey sat on his grandfather's oversized couch drinking coffee and listening to him tell the story of how his platoon had parachuted into Poland. With little to no training, he had jumped from the plane. He had walked away with a cracked ankle, but was lucky to survive. His grandfather always ended his stories just before his platoon had marched into the concentration camps and helped release the prisoners. But Aaron knew by the sad look that would sometimes cross his face, the memories were never gone.

Looking over to the mantle, he saw the row of medals lined up in a silver case and knew that his grandfather had been the reason he had become a doctor. His grandfather was the reason he now had a home, his own medical practice, and a woman who sat close by his side.

THE NEXT EVENING was the Christmas play at the grade school. Aaron sat in the small uncomfortable seat in the large auditorium. To his right was his grandfather and Betty, one of the church ladies his grandfather took a liking to, to his left was Lacey, Megan and Todd. Iian had somehow gotten out of attending the event. Aaron made a mental note to ask him how he had accomplished that feat later.

The kid's singing was tolerable, the acting was horrible, but the costumes looked great and seeing the kids in the play was priceless.

He was happy he knew most of the players because they had come into his office at one point or the other. Later he realized it wasn't the play most people came to see; it was the after-play party that was the real draw of the event.

Parents, family members, and townspeople hung out in the auditorium after the play had ended. Kids ran around free from their costumes. Cookies, cakes, and other sweets were set up along the back wall on tables. There was enough sugar to make any kid happily stick around with a bunch of adults for a few hours.

At first, he felt out of sorts as the townspeople talked and entertained each other. But soon Aaron was made to feel right at home in the large crowd. It wasn't just the fact that he was the doctor in town, but rather his grandfather's influence and the fact that Lacey and her family stood close by him.

The only parties he had ever attended had been medical-related or work-related. Only once had he attended a private party and it had ended so badly he swore off those for good.

Looking around the loud room, he realized he never wanted to leave Pride. This was truly where he belonged. His heart was bonded here and he was okay with that.

CHAPTER 13

*L*acey locked the doors and looked around the Golden Oar, which was now closed for Christmas break. She had to finish cleaning the back-dining room and she had some paperwork she'd been putting off, but then she was free. Bobby, one of the bartenders, had just left, but Iian was still back in the kitchen, cleaning up.

She headed to the shared office after spending ten minutes cleaning. She passed Iian on the way to the back and she signed, "I'm heading to the office to get some paperwork done. Are you heading home?"

"Yes, I'm beat. Don't stay too late. Are you going to be okay here?" he signed back.

She gave him a look that said, little brothers should not worry about big sisters. Of course, she was okay, this was her place, her town.

Iian headed out the back door, making sure to lock it, and spotted Aaron leaning against Lacey's sedan. He was looking up at the stars like he had all the time in the world to wait. Iian walked over to him and signed, "Waiting for Lacey?"

He really liked adding someone else in town he could

communicate with. Especially someone he liked and got along with.

Aaron signed back, "Yes, is she coming out soon?"

"No, she's doing paperwork." Aaron looked around like he was trying to decide where to go. "Come on, I'll let you in. But if she asks, you snuck in before I locked the door." He smiled.

Walking over, Iian opened the back door with his keys and held it open. Aaron gave it one look and walked in, signing, "Thank you."

Iian smiled and shut the door tightly. Lacey had been spending a lot of nights over at Aaron's lately. The old house was feeling empty but seeing his sister happy was worth it. He thought everyone should be just that happy. As he was driving by the empty antique shop, it's windows bare and dark, he thought of Allison. Another empty building, another opportunity passed by. He turned his truck uphill and headed home alone.

LACEY KNEW she was doing paperwork at midnight just to keep her mind off certain people she didn't want to think about. But damn it, his face kept popping into her mind. Why was he consuming her thoughts? Balancing books tended to help her system level off, or so she thought.

She was just starting to relax into the job when she heard a noise from the doorway. Gasping, she grabbed her stapler to use as a weapon.

"Are you trying to kill me?" she asked, trying to slow her breathing.

Aaron was leaning against the door with his arms and ankles crossed and had a smile on his face.

She wore a small black skirt with black leggings, her standard uniform top was untucked, and her shoes were on the floor next to the desk. She was holding the stapler as a weapon and if he calculated correctly, it was currently aimed at his crotch.

"How did you get in here?" she asked, giving him a questionable look.

Walking quickly to her side, he removed the stapler from her hand and placed it back on the desk.

"Let's make sure there are no work accidents here," he said as he lifted her out of the chair.

"You smell good." He leaned in, putting his hands on her small hips, and nuzzled her neck.

"Why is it," she put her hand on his shoulders to push lightly, "that whenever I ask you a question, you avoid answering?"

"Why is it, I can't keep you out of my mind?" He leaned in for the kiss, slowly, enjoying the taste of her as he ran his hands up and down her sides. "Why can't I seem to get enough of this, of you?"

He lifted her up, set her on top of the desk and her papers, making a mess of them. Standing between her legs, he let his hands roamed her body as he took the kiss deeper. He pulled her shirt all the way free and found her soft skin intoxicating. Pulling her shirt up further he started to lay kisses along her collar bone. She was warm, soft, and tasted of heaven.

She fisted her hands in his hair and pulled him closer to her heated skin with a moan. She wanted to hold him there, just there, forever.

His hands and lips were warm and roaming over her, causing little goose bumps to rise all over her body.

"I can't think when you do that." She pulled away and rested her forehead against his.

"Then don't," he said and started to kiss her again. He could feel her shaking as his hands inched under her skirt.

Pulling her up, he quickly pushed the papers aside with one quick swipe of his hand. Then he laid her down slowly on the cool surface.

She started to push him away. "Aaron? Here? Now? I can't…"

"Yes, we can. Here, now. I want you right here, right now." He was running his lips up and down her neck, kissing little trails of fire along her jaw. His hands roamed over her body and started pulling clothing aside, exposing heated skin.

"I don't think I can…mmmm," she ended on a moan as his fingers found her heated flesh. In the next moment she was gasping for air.

He enjoyed her sexy purrs as he pleasured her. He could feel the vibrations in her body as she began to orgasm. Her eyes were unfocused, and she was biting the corner of her lip just as she moaned with her release. He wanted to see her like this many more times and as many times as possible.

Standing between her legs again, he pulled her closer. He enjoyed the shocked look on her face as he plunged into her. Then she smiled seductively and wrapped her legs around him and held on.

Christmas morning was always exciting and Lacey's favorite time of Christmas day. Lacey could hardly remember a Christmas she hadn't gotten exactly what she wanted or asked for. It was easy when the thing you wanted the most was to watch your loved ones enjoy opening the gifts you had given them.

Everyone had arrived early at Megan and Todd's house for the celebration. The placed smelled like heaven, spices and evergreen mixed in the air. Since Iian had arrived a few hours earlier and taken care of all the cooking, everything was in place. This had worked out perfectly since

Lacey had been busy trying to keep Aaron away from his present.

Now with the gift safely tucked away in Megan's laundry room, she could relax before they opened gifts.

Because they were no longer children, it had been decided years ago to eat Christmas lunch first, then open gifts.

"When the baby comes along we may have to change some of our traditions." Megan said as they sat around the dining room table enjoying the food. "Kids don't like waiting until after lunch to open presents."

"I think we have another year or two before this little one will be big enough to really care," Todd said, placing his hand over his wife's growing belly.

It was always a pleasure having the family together. It was especially nice because Aaron's grandfather was there as well.

Dr. Stevens Sr. had always been a part of the town and now he was feeling like he was becoming part of their family.

"I can't thank you kids enough for inviting me today," the old man said over his second helping of sweet potatoes. "Best Christmas dinner I've had in a long time. Iian, my boy, you sure can cook."

Just then, a loud noise came from the back-laundry room.

"I'll get that," Lacey said jumping up and rushing to the back room.

A few minutes later, she came back into the room. The front of her dress was wet, and her hair was a mess, but she had a smile on her face.

"Is everything okay?" Aaron asked, starting to get up.

"Yes! No, don't get up! Yes, everything is fine." She sat down with no more explanations. How about we eat dessert after we open the presents?" The eager tone in her voice almost gave her away.

Half an hour later everyone sat around the living room in various chairs. Piles of discarded wrapping paper lay at their feet.

Megan sat with her feet tucked underneath her on the couch. Todd sat next to her, a box of baby clothes and toys next to them. Iian sat in a chair playing with his new iPad. Aaron sat on the floor next to Lacey, who had at least a dozen new brightly colored pairs of socks scattered around her. Some were from Aaron, but most were from her brothers.

Aaron's gifts were spread out on the floor like a child. He had enjoyed opening every one of them, but the one he liked the most was currently chewing on his left shoe lace.

The small brown lab puppy from Lacey had instantly won his heart. He hadn't thought he could love like this again, not after Jennifer. But with the instant pull of love and protection he felt for the small female, he knew he loved the little puppy.

"A home needs a protector." Lacey sat and watched Aaron's face. The happiness she saw there was priceless.

He'd always wanted a dog, someone he could have shared time with, someone who would have loved him unconditionally. His parents never allowed him to have a pet of any kind.

He'd been busy after graduating college, too busy to think about owning any animals then, either.

Then there had been Jennifer. She had made it very clear that owning animals of any kind were a waste of time. She had even sneered at him when he'd talked to her about getting a cat. She had said she was allergic to animals, but now he wondered how many other things she'd lied to him about.

CHAPTER 14

*T*he day after Christmas, he realized why his parents never let him own a puppy. How could something so small leak so much?

Not only did he have to let her out every half hour, but in between outdoor potty breaks, she'd taken to going on the pile of newspapers in the laundry room. However, much she peed, the play time he experienced with her made it all worth it.

She had quite an attitude and demanded his attention almost all the time. He was glad that Lacey and Bernard had spent the night again, really glad for Lacey's help in watching the puppy throughout the night.

The following morning, he tried to train her to sit. It's a simple command; he thought she could handle it. The little dog treats he tried to bribe her with weren't helping. Every time he said "sit" she would run around in circles and chase her tail instead. He was trying to be patient and was saying "sit" for the hundredth time when Lacey walked in, shaking the snow off her hat and gloves. She had walked back home to pick up a change of clothing, her snow boots, and a heavy coat.

The weatherman said they were in for more snow and to expect it to last all weekend. Lacey had told Aaron that the weatherman was wrong and that the snow was due to stop later tonight. So far, her weather predictions had been spot on, so he believed her.

"Training hard?" She gave him a sympathetic look and then laughed when the puppy rushed forward and started jumping up on her legs. "No! Down," She commanded. "Sit."

The small dog quickly stopped jumping and promptly sat on her small bottom while her tail thumped vigorously.

"How did you do that?" Shaking his head, he frowned at the small puppy. He was sure there was a conspiracy going on between the pair.

"She just needs a firm voice." She bent over and petted the chocolate fur ball. "Do you have a name yet?" The puppy quickly laid down and rolled over onto her back, exposing her belly. A trick, no doubt, learned from Bernard.

"Cleo," Aaron said as he watched the two ladies in his life.

"Cleo?"

"Her name is Cleo, after Cleopatra. She's small and demanding, but so worth it." He smiled down at the chocolate mound who had fallen asleep with all four legs in the air while Lacey continued to rub her belly.

"Cleo, what a perfect name." Lacey picked her up carefully and carried her to the doggie bed by the fireplace.

It was later, just after dinner, when the snow slowed enough to let the dogs run around the back yard. Aaron and Lacey stood watching them from his large and newly built covered deck and laughed as Cleo chased Bernard while he retrieved the ball. Cleo wasn't interested in the ball; instead she kept latching onto Bernard's ears.

Despite the extra burden, Bernard would gather the ball

and bring it back while Cleo would *retrieve* him. It was all very cute and entertaining.

Aaron had just bent down to pick up the ball for Bernard when a ball of snow landed on his neck and left shoulder.

As snow started to slide down between his collar, sending shivers down his back, he heard Lacey giggle. He grabbed a big handful of snow and retaliated.

After the great snow fight that soaked both humans and dogs, they drank hot chocolate while they sat by the fire. Their hair was still damp from the battle and they were currently snuggling in warm terrycloth robes.

One thing he could say about Lacey, she might be small, but she had a really good arm.

"I'm thinking of starting a softball team next spring and you should be the pitcher." Reaching over, he took hold of her arm and felt her tiny biceps. "How can such a small arm give such a powerful throw?"

"I grew up with two brothers. I had to know how to throw well, they ran so fast, I could never catch them. So I started throwing things at them to get their attention."

He realized she was serious and could not stop the chuckle. Hearing his laughter, she soon followed and snuggled closer to his side to feel the laughter shake his whole body. She thought she was starting to warm up and it had nothing to do with the fire.

A FEW DAYS later Aaron was a wreck. He was nervous and slightly nauseous. He knew the house was spotless, having spent most of the morning cleaning everything he owned. Why did he have so much furniture? There was a banquet of food spread out on his counter tops and even some warming in the oven. Thank goodness all the food had been delivered earlier by Iian, courtesy of the Golden Oar, so he did not have to worry about cooking. Cleo was tucked away in her kennel located in his bathroom, ensuring she did not get under any of his guest's feet at his New Year's eve party.

Lacey, however, was running late. She should have been here two minutes ago. He continued to pace in front of his front door; it wasn't like her to be late. He stopped pacing when he heard the back door open and saw her step in, shaking the snow from her coat.

"I decided to walk over, since your driveway will soon be a parking lot." She took her coat into his laundry room and hung it on the hook just inside the door. Removing her purple galoshes, she replaced them with the heels she had tucked into her overnight bag.

"I think I should have bought more beer. Should I have bought more beer? Or maybe gotten more champagne?" He was now pacing in his kitchen. Why had he agreed to a party?

"Relax, you've just the right amount of everything. Every-thing will be fine." She walked over and kissed his cheek. He looked down and noticed her then. He noticed the dress, her hair, the heels, her legs. How could he not notice her? The red dress was skin tight and hit mid thigh with a slit that traveled far enough to get his heart rate speeding to dangerous levels.

"Wow."

She stopped and smiled at him. "You like?" She did a little turn on the thin three-inch silver heels.

He started walking towards her with his mind on one thing. Her, and only her. Just as he reached her, they heard a car drive up.

"Later," he warned with a smile.

He hadn't known there were this many people in town.

There must be close to two hundred people in his house. So many that they had actually opened his back-sliding doors and people were spilling out onto his deck despite the weather. The opened doors did help in cooling off the place. Because there were so many bodies crammed in, the temperature had risen to almost blistering. The noise level was so high the music that had been playing was barely audible.

He had only seen Lacey three times since the arrival of the majority of his guests. He'd seen both her brothers several times. Todd and Megan had been sitting in the dining room with plates of food, chatting with another couple. He thought he had seen Iian talking to a tall blonde in the kitchen earlier. But Lacey was nowhere to be found at the moment.

After what seemed like his millionth conversation with one of the townspeople, he decided to look for her again.

Walking to the hallway, he heard her laughter coming from the back bedroom, along with a male voice. A long-forgotten memory surfaced.

It was a loud party, much like the one going on now. He was looking for Jennifer, to tell her… something. He didn't quite remember what it was, but he knew it had been important. He'd been looking for a few minutes now. The house had been large, the guests were spread out, and it had taken him several minutes to side step his way through the crowd. Finally, he had freed himself, so he could search some more and he remembered seeing her head up the long curved staircase, so he headed up it to follow.

Opening one door after another down the long, wide hallway had proven useless. Just as he turned to go back downstairs, he heard her laughter coming from the last door on the left which was cracked open. Walking down the hall, he reached for the door handle just as he heard a male voice.

"You aren't really going to go through with it are you? Come on, Jennifer, don't you think you've strung him along enough?"

"I know what I'm doing, Tom."

"You have to know, he'll find out sooner or later."

"It won't matter. Once I have the license, there won't be anything he can do. Besides, he's been clueless so far. I mean, he stays so busy down at the hospital. Do you honestly think he will notice? Plus, his parents are as blind as he is. They absolutely adore me and have told me I'm the best thing he has ever done."

She laughed again, but it didn't sound quite like the Jennifer he knew.

"As long as it doesn't interfere with us, I couldn't care less who you marry. I just want to know that we will still get to do this, after." It was silent then. He opened the door wider to see his fiancé and one of his best friends in a passionate embrace.

———

LACEY WAS WALKING BACK towards Aaron's bathroom just as a blonde man walked in to the bedroom. She had just taken Cleo out to relieve herself in the backyard and was returning her to the kennel.

"Well, hello again. Lacey, right?" Ric Derby walked over to the pair and gently stroked the little dog's head as she held it in her hands. Cleo wiggled with excitement at the new attention, forcing Lacey to hold on a little tighter.

"Yes, it's Mr. Derby?" She remembered, because they had briefly met at Allison's store a few weeks back. "Are you here with Allison?" She looked around.

"Yes, just looking for a place to set this down." He held up a woman's black jacket, no doubt Allison's.

"Here, let me take that for you." She quickly walked into the restroom and placed Cleo back into her kennel. The small dog began whining immediately. "Shh, shh now, settle down girl." Cleo quickly turned two circles and lay back down on her bed.

"She's cute, is she yours?" Turning, she saw that Ric was now leaning against the bathroom door with his arms crossed, much like Aaron did all the time while she did her morning ritual of hair and make-up.

"No, she's Aaron's." She walked over and held out her hands for the coat.

Ric started to hand it to her but kept a hold of it a while longer.

"Are you here with someone?" He smiled down at her.

"Yes," she laughed and said, "I'm following her lead." She nodded towards the puppy.

Ric laughed, "Why is it all the pretty one's are always taken?"

Lacey laughed again, and just then Aaron walked around the corner.

Standing in the door to his room, the memory took over again. Only this time, he saw Lacey and the man he had just been introduced to, Ric Derby. But he didn't see them standing like they were, with a few feet in between each other. Instead, he imagined them embracing. His body shook, his ears rung, and his sight dimmed.

"Oh, there you are Aaron. I was just letting Cleo out." Lacey took the coat from Ric, walked over, and hung it on a chair where other coats had accumulated.

Upon Aaron's silence, Ric jumped in. "You have a lovely home. I drove by the place just before you purchased it. It doesn't look the same." Ric noticed the man's look and the tension in the room and decided the best exit was a quick one.

Aaron had yet to say anything. Lacey noticed his hands were fisted by his sides, and there was a vibration coming from him. Walking over, she took his hand in her own. She waited for him to look at her and just looked into his eyes.

"Ric is here with Allison. Actually, he is the reason she is moving away to California." Lacey noticed his hands starting to relax in her own.

"Allison is a talented woman. I do believe she is going to make it big in the art world. Well, I better go find her." Ric quickly left the room.

"What was that all about?" Lacey turned on him the second the bedroom door clicked shut. "You were rude to Mr. Derby."

"What was that all about? What were you doing back here all alone with that man?" Aaron paced to the door and back again.

"I told you what..." she began to explain, but then she realized what the look on his face meant and where his thoughts had led him. "Is that what happened?" She walked over and took his hands again. "You've yet to open up about it. But is that what happened before? Did someone cheat on you?" She tried to look into his eyes for the answer.

He pulled his hands away and went over to the outside door and leaned his head against the windowpane, feeling the cool from the night beyond. Why was it so hot in here? He took a cleansing breathe.

She walked over and stood before him, resting her hands on either side of his face. "Aaron, look at me." She pulled his face up to her own, and he opened his eyes. "I'm not cheating on you. I would never do something like that. You are the only one I want to be with. If that ever changes, you will be the first to know. I don't play games, and I don't keep secrets."

Looking into her eyes, he could see the truth. This was Lacey, not Jennifer. Taking another breath, he pulled her close and enfolded her in his arms, breathing in her scent.

"I know, I'm sorry, I overreacted. It's just, yeah. That's how it happened. It was a hard experience to get over, the betrayal." He hugged her as she stood in front of him. She felt so right in his arms. How could he have doubted her?

"No one should have to go through something like that. I'm sorry." Just then Cleo let out a loud bark.

"Does she need to go out?" he said, his voice full of panic and concern, thinking he might have to deal with a puppy mess along with his own emotional ones.

Lacey laughed, "No, she's just being spoiled. Hearing her daddy's voice, she of course wants you."

"I like spoiling her. I like spoiling you." He reached up and kissed her slowly.

Just then, the bedroom door opened and Iian walked in with a pile of coats in his arms. Seeing them in the embrace, he quickly dropped the coats on the chair, and signed. "Get a room."

"This is a room," Aaron signed back.

Iian laughed and quickly left, making sure to leave the door wide open.

"Back to the party?" Lacey suggested.

"Fine, but later, we are going to have make-up sex." His smile was full of mischief.

"I don't think that technically qualified as an argument," she said, side-stepping away from his hold and laughing. He smiled back at her. She had a way of diffusing his moods. He really enjoyed that about her.

———

IIAN WAS out of his league. He hated, absolutely hated, parties. So why did he find himself at one of the largest ones he'd ever been to? He knew why, and she stood all five-feet, four inches tall, just inside the kitchen door. His sister had a way of making him do things he didn't want to.

He had to admit, though, he was starting to have a good time and enjoy himself. That was, until she showed up. Allison Adams walked in the front door on the arm of a tall blonde man and everything went gray. If he still had his hearing, he was sure his ears would have been buzzing at that point.

His only thought, what the hell? When he finally got his mind under control, he graduated to: Who the hell?

When the man had removed her long dark coat and he saw the little blue number she was wearing, he stopped thinking altogether.

For the past hour, he'd been avoiding the couple. Hiding out in the kitchen seemed childish, but it was better than going home early. His date for the night, Kasey, or was it Kathy, leaned against the counter next to him looking bored. It was hard for him to date since most people in Pride didn't know sign-language. But for the most part, the kind of dating he was doing didn't call for a lot of talking. Kasey was an old *"friend."* He honestly didn't know why he'd texted her and invited her along tonight. Other than the fact he didn't want to come to the party alone. Maybe that's why Allison had brought tall, blonde, and way too tan. He couldn't stop searching the crowd for the pair.

It was three minutes to midnight and his date had wandered off. He could tell she'd been mad at him for not paying enough attention to her and hiding in the kitchen most of the night. How was he supposed to pay attention to someone else when his mind was consumed with Allison?

Deciding to take a breather, he headed out to the back deck. When he realized it to was crowded, he continued down the old stone path to the side of the house. He knew there was a small cluster of trees with a swing that sat in the middle. It was hardly snowing now and the light powder covering the ground was casting a glow which helped him see his way.

Hoping no one would be there, he headed back to ring in the new year alone.

However, when he reached it, he saw a dark shadow sitting on the swing. He almost turned away before he noticed it was Allison sitting there. Looking around for her date, he realized she was alone. He must have made a sound, because just then her eyes zeroed in on him.

Stepping from the shadow of a tree, he continued towards her.

"Oh, it's you, Iian," she said, making sure to look at him.

He raised his eyebrows in question. He was an excellent lip reader but focusing on her lips seemed almost too much to handle.

"I think our dates are off somewhere together." She smiled up at him.

Nodding his head in greeting, he walked forward and stopped just in front of her, putting his hands in his pockets. He wanted to touch her so badly he had to fist his fingers to close out the want.

"Ric, he's just a friend. Actually, I guess he's going to be my new boss, since I'll be working part time at his gallery in LA." She realized she was running on, so she kicked her legs and started to swing slowly. "It's a great party. There are so many people who I'm going to miss." She took a breath and closed her eyes, raising her face to the sky. He could see her breath as she released it.

"It's cold," he said and realized he had spoken the words when she opened her eyes and stared wide-eyed at him. He had actually spoken in front of her. He didn't like speaking in front of people, especially her! But it had to be said, because she only wore a small blue strapless dress that wouldn't keep anyone warm. Walking forward, he removed his jacket and placed it gently on her shoulders.

Just then, she could hear the cheers from the house and knowing he couldn't, she stood up and turned towards him and said. "Happy New Year, Iian." She released a breath. "Will you kiss me?" she asked and waited.

How could he deny her? Why would he want to? Careful not to touch her anywhere else, he laid his lips lightly on hers and lost all his remaining senses.

She had expected it to be like before. They had been teenagers, finding their way in the dark. Now, however, it was nothing like that warm night so many years ago. He was nothing like the Iian she had known so many years ago.

The kiss lasted only a moment, but when he pulled away she was left shaking and breathless. Her lips tingled from his touch. She wanted more, much more.

"You're cold," he repeated, his voice like honey. She could get used to hearing it. "Let's head inside." He placed his arm lightly around her and walked her towards the house.

Yes, she was going to miss Pride.

CHAPTER 15

*J*anuary was flu season, which kept Aaron very busy. He'd even caught the bug himself. That's when, Lacey had officially moved into his house. She'd shown up at his door with chicken soup, hot herbal tea, and a box of her stuff. She hadn't left since that night and he didn't want her to.

It hadn't been something they discussed, it had just happened. She didn't ask for closet space or bathroom space and didn't leave her clothes lying around. She cooked, cleaned up after herself, and never asked for anything, something he had never experienced in a relationship before.

She would bring fresh flowers home every Friday to replace the ones in the vase on the mantle. She didn't complain that he never took her out to expensive places or didn't buy her expensive items.

She enjoyed staying home on cold nights and watching old movies with a big bag of popcorn and hot chocolate. She would sometimes wear a baggy sweatshirt of his and he found it very sexy.

She also helped him work on finishing the small touches

around the place he hadn't known he needed. Towels, soaps, and other small items completed his bathrooms. The magnet knife holder on his kitchen wall not only looked stylish, he now didn't have to hunt through a drawer for a sharp knife.

She also helped him train Cleo; the dog could now sit, shake, lie down, and even roll over. He was sure if they had wanted to, they could train her to do the dishes and laundry.

Before he knew it, the month had passed. He hadn't heard from his parents since the call before Thanksgiving. He doubted the silence would last much longer and didn't look forward to the scene that would unfold.

His grandfather had stopped by the home and office on several occasions. Aaron thought he stopped by the office to see Betty, rather than him. On several occasions, his grandfather had ended up taking her to lunch. It was nice to see his grandfather happy.

The weather had remained cold and wet, his yard still needed a lot of work, but it would have to wait until spring. He wanted to have a new drive poured, because the holes in his driveway were only getting bigger with the bad weather. Every time it snowed, then rained, more potholes showed up. He would have to check Lacey's car tires to make sure there was enough air in them; pot holes did a lot of damage and he didn't want her to get a flat.

Looking out his front door at the light rain hitting his mangled driveway, he waited for her to come home.

IT WAS Lacey's evening off, so she headed to her house to gather a few things she would need at Aaron's. Staying at his house every night was nice, but she still enjoyed being home, around her things. She didn't want to move everything of hers over to his place yet but had just stuck to the essentials.

Iian had given her a hard time about staying at Aaron's every night, but she knew he was happy for her. Packing another small bag, she wondered how much time she would have with Aaron.

He hadn't really opened up to her about anything from his past other than his parents, and the small bit about his break up. She still didn't know who had hurt him or the complete details that surrounded it. All she knew was that she wanted as much time with him as possible. She'd never been in a relationship like this before she wanted to know more about him, she wanted him to open up to her.

Maybe it was just a matter of time? Maybe she needed to try harder? Whatever it was, she was willing to stick around and figure it out. She'd never been so indecisive about telling someone how she felt before in her life and she didn't like it.

As she headed down the staircase, her bag flung over her shoulder, she thought about her plans for Megan's baby shower. One thing she still felt in control of was the planning and execution of her best friend's shower.

Megan and Todd were not only excited about their upcoming addition, she could tell they were getting nervous.

Running the bed and breakfast was a full-time commitment. She knew Megan enjoyed it, but Todd wasn't thrilled that his very pregnant wife was still doing a lot of the work herself. He had recently hired three local women to help out with the cleaning, cooking, and other small tasks that were required on a daily basis. Lacey could see that Megan was relieved and thankful for the help, at least temporarily. She could tell that she loved working with her guests.

Planning the best baby shower was a gift. Lacey loved planning parties, she had a knack for it. Having your own restaurant to host the party helped. It was easy to plan a surprise party because Todd kept a close eye on his wife.

Driving up Aaron's driveway, she saw him standing in his doorway waiting for her and she felt like she was home.

———

A FEW DAYS LATER, the back-dining room at the Golden Oar was decorated with pink and blue streamers and balloons. Large bouquets of flowers sat on each table along with other decorations. A banquet fit for a queen lay on a table along the back wall next to a table covered with gifts.

As guests arrived, she made sure everyone was welcomed and she placed their gifts on the table along the back wall. Everyone had a drink and people quickly paired into groups to chit-chat while waiting for the guest of honor to arrive.

She was checking with one of her wait staff, when she received a text from her brother. They were there.

"Shh, they're here," Lacey said to the crowd of women. She hadn't been this excited for someone else's party, since New Year's Eve.

Two hours later wrapping paper lay on the floor, and empty dishes were discarded on the tables. A circle of chairs sat around Megan who, in Lacey's mind, was looking a little tired and worn as she continued to unwrap gifts.

The room was loud with laughter as women of all ages watched Megan open gift after gift. There was a lot of "oohs" and "ahs" every time another bundle was unwrapped.

When the last gift was opened and passed around for approval, Lacey rolled her gift into the room. The stroller had a blue bow on top and had been special ordered from her favorite catalog.

"It's a car seat, stroller combo." She pulled the car seat off and showed her sister-in-law. "You can put the base in any car and click the carrier into it." Lacey had enjoyed picking the gift out for her soon-to-be nephew.

"It's beautiful." Megan took the blue bow and looked at it. "Something you want me to know?"

"Just my intuition." Smiling back, she gave Megan a hug and knew everything was right in her world.

It was after the party when Lacey was cleaning up in the back room, she had that nagging feeling. Stopping what she was doing, she looked around the now empty room. Setting down the tray of dishes, she headed into the main dining room just as someone shouted for help. Rushing into the front dining area, she saw Betty leaning over a figure on the ground.

Running over, she saw Dr. Stevens Sr. on the floor.

"I think it's his heart," Betty said, looking up at her.

"Quick! Call Aaron," Lacey said as she knelt down.

"Dr. Stevens, can you hear me? It's Lacey. Do you have some medication for your heart?" Lacey searched his coat pockets. Finding a bottle, she held it up. "Is this for your heart?"

The old man was conscious but looking ragged. She realized he was having a hard time breathing. Kneeling over him she placed her head on his chest and listened.

"I think he's choking!" Sitting him up and kneeling behind him, she squeezed his chest in rapid succession. It took several times before a piece of chicken dislodged and he took a breath.

"Just lay still, Aaron's on his way," she told him.

She looked up at Betty who was still on the phone. Betty nodded her head in affirmation. Holding his hand still, she leaned down and made sure he was breathing fine. Just then the front door opened, and Aaron rushed in. He saw his grandfather on the floor with Lacey leaning over him. His grandfather's color was off and for the first time in Aaron's life, he looked frail.

"Grandpa, how are you feeling?" Aaron leaned down and

placed his stethoscope against his grandfather's chest.

"He was choking," Lacey said as her hands began to shake.

Owning and working in a restaurant most of her life, she had seen several people choking before, and had even helped a few out. But this time it was different. Maybe it was because it was Aaron's grandfather. Or maybe because Dr. Stevens had always been more like a grandfather to her.

"I'm feeling better now that I can breathe. Thank you, Lacey." Dr. Stevens grabbed her hand. "Get me up off this cold floor, would you boy? I'd like to go home." He started to sit up.

"Oh, no you don't," Lacey said, trying to hold him still. "Not until you get checked out. You aren't going anywhere until he says you're clear."

Aaron smiled down at the old man. "I agree and as your doctor, I would like to examine you before I release you out into the wild."

He smiled over at Betty, who at this point was still shaken. Maybe giving her a task would help calm both of them down. "Betty can drive you over to the office."

"Come on, Gerard, you might as well not argue with those two." Betty smiled and helped him up.

"Fine, fine. Just a quick stop," Dr. Stevens said when he was on his feet.

As Betty led him out, Lacey could have sworn she saw him smiling at Betty.

Shaking her head, she realized she was still kneeling on the floor, and she started to get up. Aaron's hand was there, waiting for her. After he helped her up, he pulled her into a hug.

"Thank you," he whispered into her hair as he held onto her. He was still shaking. "I don't know what I would do without him. Or you." He released her and left to follow his grandfather.

WHEN SHE ARRIVED home that evening, she was welcomed with a wonderful smell. The house was full of flowers; they were everywhere. On the coffee table, covering the kitchen counters, the kitchen and dining room tables. The place was full of a variety of colorful bouquets.

The whole town had been talking about her. Some people had stopped in and talked to her personally, others had called. She was the local hero, the one who had saved Dr. Steven's life. She hadn't minded the attention for a while, but by the time she left the restaurant, she was over it. She just wanted to get home, relax and get off her feet. The flowers were beautiful, lifting her spirits up, making her feel wonderful. Standing in the doorway, she inhaled the wonderful smells.

"I just wanted to say thank you." Aaron stood by the fireplace. "Grandpa sends along his thanks as well. He's home resting. The ones on the table are from him."

"How is he?" She walked over to the coffee table and pushed her face into a bunch of lilacs, enjoying the smell.

"Fine, he's just fine." Walking over, he took her hand and pulled her into another hug. "Thank you, Lacey. I don't think I can ever say it enough. I'm so glad you were there."

"I'm so glad he's okay. He gave me quite a scare."

"He is my only family, family that matters to me anyway. I don't know what I would do…"

"Don't think about it Aaron. He is healthy and strong."

"You don't understand. Grandpa is the only person who has ever cared. He was the one that was there for me growing up. Every other summer was all I had with him, but he was more of a father to me than my own." Aaron walked back over to the fireplace and looked into the fire that was warming the room.

"Actually, I saw him more than my own parents. He was the one that helped me through medical school." Shaking his head clear, he focused on Lacey across the room.

Walking over to him, she reached up, kissed him and said, "I can't imagine my life without him. He was a huge part of my life." She pulled him to the couch and sat next to him.

"He was there after Iian's accident, when we lost our father. Not to mention he was always there to bandage us up while we grew up. I always thought of him more like my grandfather."

"Lacey," he pulled her into his lap, kissed her some more. "Thank you again, from the bottom of my heart. How can I ever repay you?"

"Aaron," she took his face in her hands, "you can start by taking me to bed."

CHAPTER 16

*A*aron and Lacey had just finished eating dinner. They were sitting bundled up on the back porch watching Bernard and Cleo play in the fresh snow.

"I had an interesting patient in the office today," he said.

"Mmm?" Lacey replied lazily.

"Yes, Stacie Walberg. She says she went to school with you and your brothers."

Lacey's back stiffened, her eyes turned towards Aaron.

"She's quite the talker, that one," he murmured, looking out over the yard at Bernard rolling in the snow.

"What was wrong with Stacie?" Millions of images flooded Lacey's brain.

Just then the phone rang and Lacey jumped.

Aaron was about to hit the button to send the call to voice mail when Lacey grabbed his arm and said, "Get that!" She had such a funny look on her face, he picked up the phone.

"Hello, Dr. Stevens," he paused. "When? How far apart? Yes, we can meet you, yes, she's here." Aaron handed her the phone.

"Hi, sis," Todd's voice was muffled. "You ready to be an aunt?" Lacey let out a squeak and jumped up from her seat.

"We'll meet you there." She hung up and grabbed Aaron's arm to pull him up. "Well, come on, what's taking you so long?" She tugged his arm and had him laughing.

"We have time yet; her contractions are only ten minutes apart. Come here." He had her sprawled across his lap, his mouth on hers before she could blink.

Pushing her hands up and between them, she pulled back. "How can you sit here and be so calm. A baby is coming! A Jordan baby, *come on* let's go!" She pushed harder against his chest.

"One more kiss, and I promise we'll go. Just one more... mmm," he leaned over. He hadn't realized he had needed it, but he softened the kiss, taking his time to run his lips over her soft mouth. His hands reached up and pulled her hips against his arousal.

Pulling slowly away she looked down into his eyes.

"This is no time to be starting something." She smiled into his eyes.

"Right." He stood up abruptly setting her on her feet next to him. "Let's go have a baby, shall we."

MATTHEW STEVEN JORDAN was born at 2:32 a.m. on February tenth. He weighed seven pounds eight ounces and had blond curly hair with blue eyes, which Todd swore would turn to sea green just like Megan's.

Lacey had never seen Megan smile so much, as she laughed and cuddled their new son. Lacey almost had to fight her to hold Matthew for a half hour. Between her two brothers and Megan, she was lucky she got that much time.

A few hours later, just as the sun was rising, Aaron

carried Lacey into the house. It was becoming a habit of his to carry her, one she didn't mind.

"I never thought having a baby would be so draining, and I wasn't even the one giving birth. It was amazing, I have never seen anything so… I don't know how to express it… There are no words…" she sighed into his shoulder. "Matthew is the most precious baby I have ever seen. He looks a lot like Megan, but I can see some of Todd in there as well. He looks a little like Iian when he was brought home from the hospital." Was she running on?

Aaron could hear her speech slur and smiled as she let out a yawn.

He laid her down gently on the comforter; she stretched her arms above her head. He could make out her form under the light t-shirt she was wearing.

How had it come to this? He not only wanted her most of the time, but he needed her. Needed her in his life; needed to wake up next to her, for her to be home when he got home, and to see her, to hear her, and to smell her.

He had set out to make a home for himself. Now looking around the place, he realized he had accomplished that, but the walls, paint and furniture didn't make it a home. It was the small woman lying on the bed staring up at him with big, sexy sleepy eyes and the slight smile on her lips.

"You did well today, Dr. Stevens," she said as she reached up for him.

"Hmmm… You didn't do so bad yourself. Although I think you were more nervous than Todd." He smiled remembering when Lacey had almost pulled his arm out of its socket trying to get to the hospital.

He had always wanted a family, a brother or sister to spend time with. Instead he had been shipped to boarding school after boarding school. He had never even really spent holidays with his parents.

He didn't have a home to go home to as a child, that's why he took such great stock in this place. He could imagine raising kids here in this house. He wanted to be a father. He wanted to spend his weekends wrestling with kids in the back yard, going to school plays, or just helping them with homework. Looking down at Lacey now, he could just imagine doing that with her. The idea didn't scare him like it had with Jennifer; with Jennifer he couldn't see the future. Seeing Lacey's family made him feel that the emptiness his childhood had left was now full.

"What?" Lacey said looking up at him. He had been staring into space, his eyes not focused. She leaned up and pulled him closer. "Where were you just now?"

Aaron shook his head to clear it and took a deep cleansing breath.

"Sorry, I'm back." He smiled down at her and played soft kisses along her jaw.

"Mmm, you know, someday you're going to have to talk about it." She felt him stiffen. "Aaron, I'm not pressuring you, but sometimes it's better to get it out in the open." She pulled back and looked into his eyes.

"What's in the past is done," he said simply. She pulled back further when he tried to return to her neck.

"It's not in the past if it keeps coming between us. Is it that you don't trust me? Or just the fact that this is too personal?" Lacey reached over and flicked on the bed side lamp.

"It's neither, it's just done. I don't want to talk about it." He ran his hands thru his hair and walked over to the window.

Maybe it was the nerves or the fact that he had gone almost thirty hours without any sleep or a real meal, but he just couldn't talk about Jennifer with Lacey. He didn't want something so evil to touch what they had, in any way. He didn't know how to convey this or whether he should even try.

LACEY QUIETLY GOT up and walked over to him.

When she reached up to him, he stiffened, and she quickly pulled her hand away.

"I don't mean to pry. I thought…." she trailed off, remembering the conversation yesterday before Todd's phone call. Had Aaron been hinting at something?

His shoulders were stiff and his back remained to her. She didn't know what she had thought. They had been so close the last couple of months; it was starting to feel like they had been building up to something more.

Her brothers had always warned her of getting too close, of being so trusting. Aaron had come from the city, had in fact lived in the city his whole life. He had admitted to her just a few days ago that he had only dated models, actresses, and that type of women. Maybe he was bored already. How could she compare to the life he had come from? Standing there looking at his back, things finally sunk in.

She'd been such a child; it was apparent he wanted to pull away. She could imagine he had become bored of the small-town girl. The house was done, what was to stop him from selling the place? He would make his money back for sure now that it was fixed up. Taking a step back, she turned and looked around the room. She'd been staying here almost every night for months. Was she smothering him? Did he want his space? She hadn't meant to smother him. She looked at his back again, and a little piece of her broke. It had been time to move on and she'd been so blind, a child. Well, it was time she was an adult.

Aaron had stood there looking out the window. His head

ached, and he wanted nothing more than to just make love to Lacey and fall asleep next to her. But she wanted to know about Jennifer, and that would never happen. Turning around finally, he noticed that she'd retreated across the room, her shoulders stiff in determination.

"I'm sorry, Lacey." It came out as a whisper as he started walking towards her.

"Don't." Lacey held up her hands and took a deep breath. "I understand, I'm sorry for prying. Listen, I need to get home, I forgot my uniform there. I have to be at work early for some interviews and I'm feeling just a little punchy." She tried to smile.

"Lacey, I want to explain," he tried again.

"It's not necessary." She looked around for what she thought might be the last time. "Goodnight." Turning, she walked quickly from the room.

He let her go without a word.

CHAPTER 17

*A*aron woke a few hours later to the screeching of his phone. His head hurt, his eyes stung from the lack of sleep, and his heart hurt. He answered it, mumbling a hello, and knew the day wouldn't get any better when he heard his mother's voice on the other end.

His mother told him they had just landed in Portland and were on their way down to Pride and would be there by noon. Because he had no say in it, he told her to meet him at his office. It was funny, he'd been living in Pride for almost seven months and his parents had contacted him only twice.

His parents hadn't really put any stock in his life until the last few years. He had gone to the finest boarding schools around the world and then on to the best colleges his parents' money could buy. He had worked hard all his life, trying to please his parents. Now he had moved to Pride for him, only him.

Oh, they were extremely proud when he had proposed to Jennifer. They had taken an instant liking to her; she came from the right kind of family to marry into. It seemed his mother had talked more to Jennifer on the phone than she had to him his entire life. They had flown out there several times to visit during their brief engagement.

When Aaron had broken off that engagement, he thought he would never hear the end of it from his parents. They thought Jennifer would be the best fit in the role of their daughter-in-law.

Making his way to his office, Aaron noticed Lacey's car at the Golden Oar, and felt a twinge in his chest.

He'd let her walk away because he thought it best. He wasn't in the mood to explain anything to her. Now, however, he wished he hadn't let her walk away at all.

He had a hard time getting to sleep; he kept reaching for her only to find a cold pillow. He was determined to stop by tonight and explain everything. He wanted her back at home where she belonged.

Lacey had woken up early, after a lousy night's sleep. Her eyes had been swollen and red when she'd headed into work. She got there two hours early. There was always something there she could do to keep herself busy and keep her mind off of Aaron. She had a few interviews that morning, she hadn't lied to Aaron about that. It's just that they were at eleven. She was the only one in the place this early in the morning and would be for hours. She enjoyed it, or so she told herself.

She tried to convince herself that it was better for her to walk away from Aaron, after all what did she really know about him? Sure, they had become very close over the last couple months, practically living together. But he never opened up about himself, never talked about his childhood or his past. She knew this old relationship was a big weight on his shoulders, but she knew nothing else about it.

She could tell his heart had been broken; he would some-times look off and she could see him reliving the pain. She'd hoped that one day he would open up to her, but now... She hated to think that somewhere out there was the woman he really loved, and she'd been just a rebound girl. After last night, that possibility played in her head more and more.

Iian walked in several hours later as she was filing some paperwork in the office. He took stock of her, taking in her red eyes and puffy cheeks, and had her in his arms in less than two strides. Iian had a sixth sense for these things, and she cried in his arms as he murmured comforting words into her hair. It was so nice to hear him speak, to hear his voice. Holding on to her brother, she let it all go.

AARON'S OFFICE was full of kids; evidently one of the McKenzie kids had gone to a birthday party in Portland and come back with the chicken pox. Little Susie McKenzie had then gone on a play date with Katie Norris who then passed it on to the whole church group gathered for some brunch at the church. At this point, there were about a dozen children and parents crammed into his small offices. Children with calamine lotion and runny noses, along with their worried parents sat or stood in his waiting room.

Aaron's decision to hire Betty Thomas was paying off; the older woman had quickly come in and organized his appointment books. She had a small desk shoved up against one wall in the front office and was holding a baby covered in red blotches.

Even during one of the worst days in his California offices, he hadn't had to deal with so many cases in one day. And of course, it would happen on a day in which he had only a few hours of sleep. His mind kept wandering back to Lacey and their conversation last night. He wondered why she'd backed away so quickly. Was she trying to back away from the relationship? Did she want her space? Well, she would just have to be disappointed. He had no intention of backing away or letting her back away either.

Half the waiting room was cleared out by the time his parents strolled in. He had his next patient on one of his hips, a small child covered with red blotches, her fevered head resting on his shoulder.

His mother looked perfect, of course, not a hair on her head was out of place, as usual. She had on one of her designer suits the color of pearls, a light pink jacket, and sensible heels. She was taller than most women at five-eight. Her slender build and tan face could easily be that of a model on any glamour magazine. Her medium blonde hair was styled in the latest fashion and she had on all the right jewelry, no doubt bought at Tiffany just for this occasion.

His father had always reminded him of an older version of himself with the exception that his father always looked like a GQ model in his suits. His father's hair was cut shorter than his and was always well trimmed. His blue eyes didn't miss a single detail of the room as he walked in with his wife casually draped on his arm.

He had never seen the pair wearing jeans or any other form of casual wear. Aaron had seen a picture of them once when he'd been a child; they were on a beach somewhere tropical and both clad only in bathing suits. He remembers thinking that it could have easily been a professional shoot for a bathing suit commercial.

But what really shocked him was the woman who stood behind his father's left shoulder.

She was taller than his mother, thinner, and looked like she'd just walked off the catwalk. Her longer blonde hair ran down her back in a wave. She had on one of those smiles that didn't quite reach her eyes, eyes that were scanning and criticizing everyone and everything. Aaron's back stiffened, and his headache tripled.

Just then the small child in his arms lifted her heated head from his shoulder and groaned.

"Aaron, what are you doing here?" His mother asked when she looked around at the room of crying, itching children.

Handing the child to Betty, he said. "Please take Melissa and her mother to room three. I won't be long." Then he said to his mother, "Hello, Mother, please come back to my office." He walked the trio to the back room.

As soon as the door was closed, he rounded on them, but before he could get out a word, his mother interrupted.

"You go away for a week sabbatical and we find you living here. Jennifer was worried, we haven't heard from you in almost eight months. We show up to find you doing God only knows what. Really Aaron, we raised you above all this." She was waiving her hands around the room.

Jennifer stood in the background, twisting the engagement ring she'd refused to return when he'd called it off. She kept her eyes on his parents and refused to meet his glare.

"Mother, what I do is no concern to you. I've been here almost a year with only two calls from you and one was just today. I've left several messages for you on your voice mail with no return calls. I'm living here now and have taken over Grandpa's practice for good. I have a house, a practice, and no intentions of having that woman in my life anymore." He pointed to the corner where Jennifer stood.

"You know we broke it off last year. Why would you bring her here?" He paced the small room.

"Aaron, you mind your tone with your mother," his dad piped in. "You've had quite enough fun here, and it's time you went back to your responsibilities. If LA won't work for you, I've made arrangements for a new position at the Thomas

Jefferson University Hospital in Philadelphia. I pulled a few strings to get you an excellent position. Jennifer is excited about the move as well and has arranged for all your things to be shipped." His father walked over and patted Jennifer's hand. "She's been instrumental in the whole process."

"What? What? I can't believe what I'm hearing," Aaron rubbed his forehead. "What part of *'Engagement called off'* do you people not understand?" His voice grew louder.

"I agreed to your visit, Mom and Dad, however after listening to this, I want you to leave. I can't handle you here right now." He rounded on Jennifer. "And you knew what my reaction would be before you stepped foot in Oregon. What did you think would happen?"

Jennifer had been hiding behind his parents. Now the whole room turned to look at her.

"Aaron, I know we had an argument, but it was foolish. I'm sure you didn't mean the things you said, and well, I was upset at you and said some things back. Your parents are right; won't you listen to them? This position in Philadelphia is just what we need, a new beginning. You should see the facilities there." She walked over and tried to reach for his hand. "Oh, Aaron, you will love it and your parents have found the perfect little house for us." She ignored his glare and tried to continue.

"Out." It was no more than a whisper but cut the silence.

Just then there was a quick knock and Betty's head peaked in quickly. "Sorry to interrupt. Melissa and her mother are waiting in room three, Johnny Cavanaugh and his mother are in one, and the whole Miller family is in two." Then, just as quickly her head disappeared, and the door closed.

"I won't have you talking to your fiancée and mother this way. You have responsibilities, Aaron; it's time you grew up.

We'll be staying at your Grandfather's place. I expect you to be there for dinner tonight, so we can discuss this further."

With that, the group walked from his room. Aaron grabbed the first thing handy and threw it at the closed door and then he went over and sat behind his desk. He put his head on the cool wood and wished more than anything he'd never agreed to their visit.

CHAPTER 18

The Golden Oar was full, thanks to the noon rush. Lacey saw a party of three walk in and almost had to do a double take. At first, she'd thought it was Aaron that had walked in a blonde on each arm. When she looked more closely she saw it wasn't Aaron, but a man who looked so much like him, she could only assume it was his father. She felt a twinge in her chest; his parents had been planning a trip and he hadn't told her.

She knew he wasn't close to them, but she felt that if she had meant something to him, he would have told her. This just confirmed for her that it was truly over between them.

Of course, they were seated in her section. On approach she heard the young blond asking Aaron's parents if they wanted to eat somewhere nicer. Lacey felt an instant dislike for the woman.

She also felt intimidated, noticing the perfection of the trio. All of them were tall. Aaron's father had a few gray hairs around his forehead, and she saw that he had smaller shoulders; and he was a little leaner than Aaron.

His mother was tall, thin, and tan; she could easily have

been a model. Lacey could see Aaron had inherited his mother's mouth and chin.

The other woman who was with them was a complete mystery. To say that she was gorgeous was an understatement. Not a single hair was out of place and her simple dress looked exotic. Lacey looked down at her black skirt and her red and white striped shirt with a wine stain on the front and felt even plainer than before. She was sure her eyes were still puffy from the night's cry.

So, this is what Aaron came from? Well, they could have him back. Raising her chin, she walked over.

"Hello, my name is Lacey, have you had a chance to look over the menu?" The younger woman didn't even look up at her, but just smirked at the front cover of the menu, which Lacey's brother Todd had drawn years ago.

Aaron's father ordered first, ordering the most expensive steak, followed by Aaron's mother, with a chicken salad, then the other woman who only ordered a "clean" salad.

Lacey placed their orders in the computer and told Julie her trainee, to take her half hour lunch. She felt a larger headache coming and didn't want the girl to take the brunt of her anger.

When she'd delivered their food, the young woman had looked down her nose at the crisp fresh salad and made a face as if she had smelled something foul. Lacey ignored it and smiled at her.

As she was leaving the table, she overheard some of their conversation. Lacey desperately wanted to eavesdrop, so she made sure all the customers on either side had their waters full, taking her time as she went.

"Really, Jennifer, you know what's going on here... It's the last fling before the wedding. Aaron will enjoy the move to Philadelphia and before you know it, the director's chair will be his. You'll see, a fall wedding in Philadelphia is just perfect." Lacey heard Aaron's mother saying.

Lacey looked over and saw the woman, Jennifer, twisting a diamond ring around on her finger and then for the first time in Lacey's life, everything went white and she passed out.

Lacey woke in warm arms and felt awake enough to know that her brother was screaming at her. That in itself was a strange thing because there were other people present. Iian never really spoke in public, let alone screamed.

When she finally opened her eyes, she could see she'd been moved to his office couch. "Damn it, Lacey, come on…. Go call the doctor," he yelled at someone.

That was enough to startle her completely awake and she pushed Iian away enough to sit up.

"No! Don't call the doctor! I'm perfectly fine." She pushed herself into a sitting position.

Frustrated, Iian signed to her, "What the hell are you doing? I'm taking you over there myself. You're as pale as death. What's wrong?"

Signing back, she told him everything. By the time she'd finished, she could see he was steaming.

Iian asked Katie to finish training the new staff and demanded that Lacey take the rest of the day off. Someone had called Todd, because when she walked outside fifteen minutes later, he was just pulling up; he rushed forward and enclosed her in a firm hug.

"What the hell are you doing scaring us like that?" He pulled back to take a better look at her. Noting her pale face and the dark circles under her eyes, he barked at her. "You aren't pregnant, are you?" She could see the anger growing in his face.

If she hadn't been so tired she would have laughed.

"No, I'm not pregnant. I just haven't gotten a lot of sleep

with us at the hospital until late, and Aaron and I sort of had a fight." She pulled away as the front door opened and the trio came gliding out. She'd almost forgotten about them. Her back stiffened as she looked at Jennifer again.

Todd noticed her gaze and reaction, quickly putting a protective arm around his sister. He looked at the three-people coming out of the restaurant. Instantly he recognized Bradford Stevens. He'd met him several years back.

Mr. Stevens stopped when he saw Todd. "Oh, hello Todd." He walked over and gripped Todd's hand in a firm hand shake. "It's good to see you again. I'd forgotten you lived around here." Mrs. Stevens walked over as well.

"Todd, this is my wife, Elizabeth. This is Todd Jordan, owner of Jordan Shipping. We met a few years back at a conference in Singapore."

"Nice to meet you. I didn't know you were in town." Todd tightened his hold a little on Lacey when she tried to squirm away.

"Oh, we're just here for about a week visiting our son, Aaron," Aaron's mother chimed in.

Todd's mind sharpened, he'd pieced it together when he'd met Bradford that he was Dr. Steven's son. Suddenly things began coming together for Todd. He had forgotten that Bradford Stevens was Dr. Stevens son, and therefore, Aaron's father.

Just then another woman walked up to stand next to them.

"Todd, this is Jennifer Andrews, Aaron's fiancée. Jennifer, Todd runs a very prominent shipping company, one of last year's Fortunes 500 companies, if my memory serves me," Bradford said.

Lacey felt a shiver down her back; she took a quick peek at Jennifer and could almost see dollar signs in her eyes.

Todd's arm tightened when he heard the words, "Aaron's

fiancée". If Lacey knew anything about her brother, she knew that right about now, Todd was thinking of a million ways to kill the town's doctor. Reaching up, she put a protective arm around her brother, restraining him.

"Oh," Todd said under his breath. "I didn't know Aaron was engaged." Lacey heard the heat in the statement and nudged her brother. "Pardon my rudeness, Mr. & Mrs. Stevens, this is my sister Lacey. She owns and runs the Golden Oar."

Lacey nodded to the pair. They looked her over from head to toe. It was obvious that they had been present during her fainting spell. Embarrassment caused her face to flush. Aaron's father took her small hand. "Oh, yes, how are you dear? That was a nasty spill you had in there." Aaron's mother gave her no more than a quick nod.

"If you will excuse me, I need to get my sister home. It was nice seeing you again." Todd turned, keeping Lacey close, and walked them to his car.

Once inside, she laid her head back on the head rest and silently cried. Todd, being the kind brother, he was, let her cry it out.

When he stopped the car a few minutes later, she noticed that it was at his house instead of hers.

"Todd, I just want to go home," she began.

"No, I'm not letting you deal with this alone. He fooled us all, Lacey. I'm not going to leave you by yourself during this. Besides, I'm going to go pick up Megan and the baby from the hospital soon, and I know she would really enjoy the help and company."

Lacey ended up staying the night at Todd and Megan's. Little Matthew and the company of her family were a comfort to her. She cooked them all dinner and fell asleep on their couch. When Todd carried her to their extra bedroom, she woke and cried silently most of the night.

WHERE THE HELL WAS SHE? Aaron wondered, sitting outside her house. Her car was still at the restaurant, but someone had said she'd left hours ago. Bernard was curled up on the doormat waiting, too. He was sure she was upstairs ignoring him. At one point he thought about climbing up a wall to peek in the high windows.

Didn't she know what she was doing to him? It had been murder not having her there last night, and he was unsure whether he could go without her another night. He sat there in his truck watching the rain pour off his windshield until he saw headlights in his rear-view mirror. It was a quarter to one in the morning. But instead of Lacey, Iian got out of the sedan.

Iian rushed to Aaron's door, pulled it open, and had Aaron out of the truck by his jacket so fast he didn't have time to respond.

"What the…" Aaron didn't get a chance to finish before Iian's fist plowed into his face, snapping his head back against the door.

Aaron had taken several beatings from bullies while in boarding school, but this one had more power and feeling behind it than any he'd ever felt before. Putting up his hands, he stopped the next blow and then pushed Iian back a few feet. He quickly signed. "What was that for?"

Iian signed back, "You know what that was for. That's for Lacey and the next one is from me." He began to swing again, but Aaron was ready and dodged the blow.

He signed again, "Hang on a minute." Then he yelled, "Hold on!" When Iian swung again.

"What's going on? Where's Lacey?" he signed quickly when Iian stopped swinging.

"She's somewhere you can't get to her again," Iian signed

back. "You need to just leave her alone. If you ever come near her again…"

"What do you mean?" Aaron interrupted. "I haven't done anything to her."

"You're engaged, or did you forget?" Iian signed.

Aaron took a step back and leaned against his car door, his face turned white. Iian could see the shocked look on his face. Aaron's left eye was starting to swell and Iian felt a little pride knowing the doctor would soon have a black eye.

"No," Aaron said out loud.

"No, what?" Iian signed. "No, you didn't forget? Or no, you're sorry Lacey found out about it? You used my sister." It made Iian so mad he started to take a step towards Aaron again, maybe to blacken the other eye, when Aaron said, "No, I'm not engaged." Aaron had said it rather then signing it, and because it was fairly dark out with the only light coming from the front porch, Iian had to sign and ask him to repeat his last statement.

"I was engaged last year, to Jennifer. I broke it off shortly after. I'm not engaged to her and would never marry her. I'm in love with your sister." Aaron signed.

Iian took a step back, looked deep into the doctor's eyes and saw the truth. Then he let out a bark of laughter and punched the man's arm brotherly.

He signed, "Well, I guess you better come in and explain it all and maybe put something on that eye," he smiled.

LACEY WOKE in the spare bedroom at Todd and Megan's. She took a deep cleansing breath and opened her eyes, then screamed when she saw a man sitting over her looking down into her face. It took a second for her to realize it was Aaron.

"Sorry," he mumbled and started to move back.

She swung out and caught him on the chin. He fell backwards off the side of the bed, hitting his head on the dresser. He let out of string of low curses while rubbing the side of his head.

"Out! Get out!" Lacey gathered the pillows, and standing on the bed, began throwing them in his direction. "Now! Get out now!" She threw the next thing she could grab a small alarm clock hit the dresser just above where his head was.

"Damn it, Lacey, would you stop for just a minute?" He rushed over and grabbed her, flipping her over so that she lay underneath him. Her chest rose and fell with quick breaths.

"Get off me," she said under her breath, trying to push him away with her legs. She tried to twist and get her hands free from his iron hold.

He could see the tears building up in her eyes, eye's that had dark circles under them and were puffy.

"I am not engaged to Jennifer, anymore! I broke it off before I moved here," he blurted out.

She stopped fighting and looked at him for the first time. His left eye was swollen and purple, and he had a fat lip.

"What?" she asked, taking it all in.

"I'm not engaged, period!" he said, holding her down and enjoying the feel of her under him. She was wearing a large white T-shirt and gray sweat pants.

"Oh, then why…?" she trailed off.

"I don't know why my parents and Jennifer won't accept that I called it off. They won't leave me alone about it. She still has the stupid ring I bought her. I think they're all delusional. The only one I want to be with now is you. Just you," he said, smiling down at her.

She took a few deep breaths to steady herself.

"Did I do that to you?" she nodded towards his eye and lip.

He released her with one hand and touched his eye lightly.

"No, the eye is from Iian, the lip is from Todd. But from what I hear, I can see why they thought I deserved it. Listen, I should have told you earlier, I guess I just…"

She reached around with her free hand and pulled him down into a kiss. She wanted to show him everything that she'd been feeling the last day, the hunger, the loneliness, and the want.

She was soft and warm and smelled and tasted like home. He couldn't get enough. He reached under the light shirt and touched her soft skin. He heard a moan and realized it was his own. He pulled her hand and that had been desperately trying to untuck his shirt from his pants, above her head to join her other one.

"Lacey," he said, breathing hard. "Your family is downstairs." She ran kisses up and down his neck, causing small bumps to rise on his arms. He was shaking so bad, he thought everyone in the house would feel it.

"They won't mind, let me just…mmmm," she said taking his ear lobe into her mouth, causing his eyes to cross. She was moving underneath him again, this time in a slow, more sensual rhythm. He knew they needed to finish talking and he couldn't concentrate if they stayed in their current position. He pulled her up to a sitting position quickly before he could change his mind.

Turning her towards him, he continued. "Lacey, I should have told you from the start. I'm sorry I let things get this way." He looked down at their joined fingers. They were both breathing hard.

"I asked Jennifer to marry me early last year, but we were only engaged for a few months. I caught her with a coworker of mine at a friend's party and I called it off." He took a deep breath, trying to steady his breathing.

"I overheard her saying that she was just marrying me for my money and that they would continue their affair after the marriage." He looked up into her eyes. "I thought she'd broken my heart." Lacey reached up and placed her hand on his cheek.

"My parents don't know the whole story. All they know is that I called it off, and a few months later moved here. They think all of this is some kind of sabbatical."

Lacey remembered his parent's words at the restaurant and heat flooded into her face.

"I thought…" she began.

"I know what you thought, and I'm sorry," he began.

"No, let me finish." She stood up and walked to the window looking out at the back yard. She watched Todd, Megan and the new baby strolling around the back yard in the sun and smiled.

"I thought you were done with me." She turned back to him and could see the hurt cross his eyes. "I'm inexperienced in all this," she waved her hands about. "I thought you were done and then when I overheard your parents and…" Lacey stopped. She couldn't even say her name. "I don't know how to deal with this," she stammered.

Aaron stood, walked over and laid his hands gently on her shoulders. "Lacey, I'm sorry I didn't open up to you sooner. This is entirely my fault; I'll never forgive myself the hurt I've caused you. I'm not done with you, I don't think I could ever be done with you. I was building up enough courage to tell you that I've fallen in love with you, and I blew it. Maybe we can start over?" He felt her stiffen and he reached around and pulled her tight against him.

"Lacey, I can't go another day without you. I love you and want to be with you," he murmured into her hair.

"I…mmmm," she smiled into his chest. She heard his

heart skip a beat and could tell he was holding his breath waiting for a response.

Pulling back, she looked into his eyes and smiled. "I love you, too. It was killing me thinking that you were over me." She hugged him again. "And then it killed me further thinking that I'd been your rebound girl."

He chuckled, then pulled her back to him. "You are not my rebound girl. You are much more than even I had dreamed. When I came to Pride, I was broken. You did more than fix me, you made me see for the first time in my life what it was I truly wanted." He kissed her softly, her cheeks wet from tears. He kissed each eye and gently wiped away each drop.

"And what is it that Doctor Aaron Stevens truly wants?" she smiled up into his face.

"You, just you," he said again and claimed her mouth once more, running his hands down her back. When she'd melted completely against him, he pulled her closer.

She arched towards him and ran her hands up to grip his hair, pulling him closer.

"Ouch!" He pulled back, releasing her to rub his head where he had hit it on the dresser just five minutes before.

"Oh, Aaron, I'm sorry." she pulled his head down to her level to look at the small bump that had started to form.

"You know, I've been hit by almost every member of the Jordan family today. Now all I need is for Megan and the baby to clock me." He smiled.

"The day is still young," she said, smiling back at him.

He laughed. "I have to go into the office," he frowned down at her. "My parents and Jennifer are still in town and I have to deal with them once and for all. Will you be coming home tonight?"

"Yes." She liked how he had said that. She really did think of his home as her's now.

Lacey quickly changed her clothes and they headed downstairs, just as Iian came out of the kitchen with a plate of food. He set it down at the table for the guest at Megan's bed and breakfast and signed.

"Everything get straightened out?"

"Yes," both Lacey and Aaron said, smiling.

"I'd better go get ready. I've an early day, there are more chicken pox cases coming in. But I can see if I can break for lunch. Can I see you for lunch?" He pulled her close.

"I'll save the best table for you." She smiled back and kissed him quickly.

After Aaron left, Lacey headed over to his house to shower before heading into work herself. She was sure her brothers were both happy to have the situation resolved. She knew they would do anything for her but seeing the marks on Aaron's face had just confirmed it. Not that she ever condoned violence, but in this case, she couldn't help feeling more pride than anything.

WHEN AARON WALKED into the clinic, he had expected to see the waiting room full. He hadn't however, expected to see Jennifer sitting in his office with her hands folded in her lap.

He crossed the room without saying anything and sat behind his desk.

"You didn't show up for dinner last night," she said in a bored tone. Then seeing his face she stood. "Oh Aaron, what happened to your face?" She started walking forward.

Aaron put up a hand to stop her, then touched the swollen eye and shrugged. "A misunderstanding, nothing too serious." He sat behind his desk and took a deep breath. "Jennifer, it's time you stopped playing these games."

When she said nothing, he continued. "Go home. You know you don't belong here."

"Aaron, I'm truly sorry about the party. I never meant any of it. You have to understand, I was under a lot of pressure with the wedding plans and your family. Brett was just a distraction, he never really meant anything and well… It only happened the one time and we called it off. Can't we just forget it ever happened?" She stood up and walked over to his side of the desk, leaning against his chair.

"We can start over in Philadelphia, a new life. The job your father has lined up will make us both happy. There was that cute little house just outside of the city. Oh, Aaron," she tried to grab his hand, but he pulled away. "We can start a family." She looked down at him.

He saw it then, in her eyes, the desperation.

"Why are you here, Jennifer? Don't lie to me." He stood and looked at her.

Her eyes started flooding with tears and he could see there was no real emotion behind them. Had he ever really fallen for her tricks? She was as transparent now as an x-ray.

"Aaron, can't we make it work? I've given you so much of my heart, my time; we have to make this work." She began to pull closer to him.

"Jennifer, it's over, it's been over. Not only do I not believe you, I no longer care. I've moved on. I have someone in my life now, and now you need to move on. It's time you went home and left my parents out of your schemes. Just go." He grabbed the files off his desk and walked out, leaving her staring after him.

JENNIFER STOOD THERE for a full minute, letting his words sink in. How could he do this to her? She had taken so much time tracking him down two years ago, when she had walked into his hospital. She had researched who he was, finding out everything she could about him. She had planned and planned and finally he had noticed her. She'd given up everything for him.

She had been stupid that night at the party when he had caught her with Brett, one of her many lovers. She had a few men that helped her pay her rent, her car payments, and her other bills. Brett had followed her into the back room and she was caught off guard when Aaron had walked in. She was sure Aaron would believe her when she accused Brett of molesting her, but apparently, he had overheard part of their conversation and had immediately called off the wedding.

All her carefully laid out plans had been ruined. Then Aaron stopped returning her calls and when she had tried to go see him, his doorman wouldn't let her in. She had tried to see him at work, but they had told her he had quit. She tried everything she could think of, day after day. Then days turned into weeks and after a whole month went by, she had almost given up. But then his parents had called her; they hadn't heard the news of the break up. She played it up to them that they had moved the wedding date back six months due to Aaron's new schedule at the hospital and the next thing she knew, she was on a flight to visit them in London.

Her in London! She'd never been out of California before. Then she was traveling with them to Greece, where they purchased a wedding dress for her. She'd spent three months traveling with his parents, not once mentioning to them that the wedding had been called off.

When, she finally told his parents something, all she had said was that they had a small fight. She had shown them just the right amount of tears and they had believed her. It was actually quite easy for her to play the role. If she looked at it, it actually was more Aaron's fault than her own. After all, she'd tried to rectify the situation, but he hadn't wanted anything to do with her. If she'd just had an opportunity to explain, she was sure he would have taken her back. Even now she was sure Aaron would take her back if he would just listen.

What had he said about seeing someone else? She had to find out who he was seeing. Walking slowly out of his office, she turned towards the front office and saw the old woman sitting behind a small desk.

Jennifer was sure she could get any information she needed out of the old hag. She would just have to make Aaron see how serious she was about winning him back.

EVEN THOUGH LACEY had only slept for four hours last night, she felt better today. Her mind was so much more at ease; she knew she could sleep for hours as long as it was next to him. Just knowing that everything was better between them gave her a little bounce in her step. She smiled a little brighter knowing that he loved her and that he knew that she loved him back.

After finishing with a smaller lunch group, she watched Jennifer walk in the doors, all alone this time. Lacey thought she'd come to grab another clean salad, but, instead of stopping at the front desk, she marched over to Lacey with her fists clenched.

"Just who do you think you are?" she said in a loud voice, which rang out across an empty dining hall.

"I beg your pardon?" Lacey asked, watching several of the locals turn towards the pair. "You're Jennifer, right? Maybe we should head in the back to my office for a minute?" Lacey tried to start walking towards the double doors.

"You think he really wants you? You're just a stepping

stone, a distraction." She waved her arms, not caring who saw or heard. "He could never stay here, this is all beneath him. I mean, just look at this place." She waved her arms again. "Do you really think he could live in a place like this for too long? With someone like you? I'm warning you, stay away from him. He needs some time to realize that this isn't what he wants. We're going to move to Philadelphia where he's going to be the director of a very large and prestigious hospital. We have a mansion that's just waiting for us; we'll be married this fall." She stepped forward, putting her face so close that Lacey could see the specks in her blue eyes. "You think he would stay here with you? He's done with you! What we have is forever! You're just entertainment, something to warm his bed. You're just another slut, a notch on his bed post."

Lacey had listened quietly and patiently through the woman's rant, but with the last statement, she found her hand raised and before she knew what she'd done, a loud slap rang out and echoed in the room.

Jennifer stood with her hand over her left cheek, a shocked look on her face. Lacey took a deep breath.

"If you're done, you can leave my restaurant. You're not welcome back." Lacey turned and without looking back, walked into the back rooms, shaking. It had taken every ounce of courage not to argue with the woman. She'd acted like a spoiled child who wanted what the other kids had, nothing more.

She didn't deserve Lacey's time. So why was it so hard to get the vicious words out of her mind?

———

LESS THAN HALF AN HOUR LATER, Jennifer walked into Aaron's office again. This time, she didn't wait patiently in his office;

instead she screamed and cried until he came out of a patient's room, concerned that someone was seriously hurt. When he spotted her standing at the front door with Betty desperately trying to calm her down, he knew there was no stopping the scene that would follow.

"She hit me!" Jennifer screamed. She was holding her left check, which was a mean shade of dark purple and extremely swollen.

Betty piped in. "Who hit you?"

Jennifer didn't even glance at the older woman before screeching out. "That whore, Lacey Jordan. She hit me in front of everyone in that garbage pile she calls a restaurant." Jennifer ran forward and threw herself at Aaron's chest, weeping deeply into his shoulder.

CHAPTER 19

egan had enjoyed a quiet day at home with her new son Matthew. Todd had woken early with a phone call and a much-needed trip into the office. With the promise of a family lunch at the restaurant, she'd been enjoying having Matthew all to herself. This was to be her first real outing with the baby. Looking into the rear view mirror at her little bundle strapped in to his car seat made her smile.

She enjoyed dressing her little man in one of his new jumpers. This was Matthew's second car trip since returning home yesterday, and so far he looked like he was enjoying it. With him tucked into his car seat and sleeping quietly, she pulled into the parking lot of the Golden Oar.

Just as they arrived, a woman with long blonde hair came running out of the restaurant doors. She looked around frantically, then she walked over to a slick silver car parked in the lot. She opened the door and violently struck her face with it over and over with her own car door. Megan was so taken back by the woman's action, she never once thought to stop her.

The woman kept opening and closing the door on her own face until her left check was swollen and red. Megan could see the purple mark on the woman's face as she drove away.

Having come from years of abuse, at the hands of her ex-husband, she'd witnessed firsthand the horrors of being slapped around. For a woman to do this kind of damage to herself just confused Megan.

She must have sat there for about five minutes thinking about what she'd just seen. Finally, she heard a knock on her window. Todd stood just outside the Jeep smiling at her. When he opened the door, she jumped out and said, "You will never believe what I just saw."

AARON WAS HAVING a hard time calming Jennifer down. It appeared she'd called his parents, because not two minutes after she came running in, both of them ran in his office doors. He had just gotten Jennifer into one of his empty rooms to take a look at her face, when they stormed in.

"We need to call the police," his mother said after seeing Jennifer's swollen face. "This is outrageous! Bradford, give the local sheriff a call now. I want this woman charged." She rushed over to Jennifer's side holding her hands in her own.

Aaron found it funny that not once in the last few minutes had his parents asked him about his bruised and swollen face.

Aaron wasn't sure what had happened at the restaurant, but he couldn't believe Lacey would have done such a thing. While his parents hovered over Jennifer, he excused himself and called over there to find out what had happened.

After talking to Todd for about five minutes, he slammed down the phone. He was as angry as he'd ever been. He tried to calm down. He even took several cleansing breaths as he made his way back to the room where his parents, Jennifer, and now the local sheriff, Robert Brogan, were. The sheriff was standing there writing notes on a small pad, and when Aaron walked in, the officer looked him over.

"Dr. Stevens, may I ask how you got that black eye and fat lip?" He took a step-in front of Jennifer.

Obviously, Aaron could see the connection the man was making.

"My face has nothing to do with what's going on here. But I can tell you this." He touched his eye. "I received these last night from two different people and no," he held up his hand when he saw what the officer was thinking, "I don't want to press charges." Aaron walked over to his parent's side and looked at Jennifer.

"Before you go any further in this investigation, I believe there are a few people in the front office that would like to speak to you." Sheriff Brogan looked up from his pad with a questioning look.

"It does pertain to what transpired at the Golden Oar." Aaron left it at that. Both the Sheriff and Aaron's father followed him into the waiting room, which Betty had cleared out of waiting patients after rescheduling every appointment for the following day.

Megan sat holding Matthew; Todd, Iian and seven other people were crowded into the small room, all standing protectively around Lacey.

Sheriff Brogan approached and nodded at the brothers. "Afternoon, Lacey. I hate to do this, but that young lady in the other room wants to press charges. Unless I have witnesses saying otherwise," he looked at the group of people. "I'm going to have to take you to my office to get this matter cleared up." He began walking towards her.

"You will do no such thing!" Everyone looked around the room to see who had spoken.

Megan stood up holding little Matthew in front of her. She handed the baby to her husband, then she walked over and stood in front of Lacey, shielding her.

"What I've witnessed today is the information you need."

Fifteen minutes later when they walked back into the small exam room, Elizabeth was still coddling Jennifer, whose face had turned an even darker shade of purple. She held a small ice pack on her cheek.

"Elizabeth, I think it's time we left," Aaron's father said harshly. Without waiting for a reply, he walked over and grabbed his wife's hand then walked her out of the room as she sputtered questions.

"Miss Andrews, some witnesses have stepped forward with more information about what happened at the Golden Oar. No charges will be pressed against Lacey Jordan at this time, and I'll file this report as negligent. If you have any further questions, please feel free to call our offices." He handed her a card and without saying anything further, walked out of the office.

"What? What just happened? I want that woman in jail where she belongs. What are you doing?" She stood and started to follow the sheriff.

Aaron reached over and grabbed her arm. "No! Jennifer, your games won't work here. Someone saw what you did." The simple statement stopped her.

"What I did?" She yanked her arm away from him.

"How you did that." He pointed towards her face. "You must be very desperate to do something like this." He crossed his arms over his chest.

"I don't know what you're talking about. I got this from her." Jennifer pointed to the open door. Lacey stood just outside, looking in. "I've told you what happened. Ask anyone in that place, they'll tell you; she hit me." Her voice had gotten louder, and it came out as a screech.

"Someone saw you, Jennifer. It's over, go home. For God's sake, get out of my town." Aaron walked out the door and, grabbing Lacey's hand, said softly. "Come on, Lacey, let's go home."

LATER THAT NIGHT as they lay in bed, the dogs lying on the foot of the bed, they talked. Aaron told her the full story of his relationship. As the fire started to die in the fireplace, every detail of the break-up came out.

He didn't hold anything back. His feelings, his pain, his anger, everything was out there for her to see. Looking over at her, the firelight in her hair, he reached over and pushed a strand of dark hair off her forehead. Her crystal eyes reflected the lights and sparkled. He realized he trusted her completely. But more importantly, he realized he loved her, loved her like he had never loved anyone before.

"I meant it, you know." He turned onto his side to get a better look at her.

"What?" she turned to face him.

"I do love you." This was met with silence. Reaching up, he wiped a tear from her cheek.

"Lacey?"

"No, ssh," she touched his mouth with her fingers. "I just want to lay here, listen to the rain, hear the dogs sleeping by our feet, and hear you say it again. Please say it again, Aaron."

He smiled and pulled her closer. Kissing her forehead, he said it again. "I love you with all of my being."

CHAPTER 20

*I*t had been three days since she'd been humiliated. She was getting more upset every time she thought of it. She had been trying to call the Stevens', but they were no longer returning her calls. She made sure to leave long voice messages explaining how everyone had lied to cover up what had really happened, thinking that if she just had a chance to talk to them and explain everything, they would come to see her side. But when she got back to the old man's house, no one answered. She stayed there, parked in her rental car for almost two hours, and no one came back. She was about to drive away, when she saw the old man drive up.

He told her that he'd just dropped Bradford and Elizabeth off at the airport an hour ago.

They had left her here!

What she hadn't told anyone was that she was broke. She had quit her job after Aaron's parents had contacted her and she'd been living off of them for the last few months.

How was she going to get home? To what home was she going to go? She knew the rental car she was driving was under their name, so she was safe to keep it as long as she wanted.

How was she supposed to live?

She looked around after Dr. Stevens left her standing in the rain. She'd banked everything on Aaron taking her back. She wasn't about to lose; it was time for drastic measures!

LACEY HAD SPENT every night at Aaron's place since his parents had left town. They had spent almost an hour talking to them before they'd left. They had apologized several times to both Lacey and Aaron, for their part in Jennifer's scheme. They'd agreed to spend their summer break, a whole week, in Pride.

Aaron had gone out of his way the last few days to spend as much time with Lacey as possible. They'd taken the dogs on evening walks almost every night.

Aaron had made a point to show up every day when she worked the lunch shift, but today he was too busy to get away. He hated to call off lunch, especially since it was Valentine's Day, but at least he had planned a nice quiet dinner for later that evening.

When Aaron called off lunch, Lacey decided to take her lunch break and deliver some sandwiches to him, instead.

Stepping outside just as the rain started, she realized she loved living in Oregon. Most people who lived here tolerated the weather. Lacey lived for it. Ever since she was little, the rain had been more soothing to her then anything.

As she drove through town, she realized the people in Pride never really ran indoors when it rained. The three old men still sat out on the bench smoking their cigars in front of the barber shop, safe from the rain under its large porch. There were people standing in front of the market under the awning. And as she pulled up to Aaron's office, she saw Betty heading out the door towards her car with a red umbrella.

Parking her sedan across the street, Lacey tucked the sandwiches under one arm and a thermos of tomato soup in the other. She was heading for the door when she heard the squeal of tires. By the time her head snapped up, there was no time to do anything but scream.

AARON HAD BEEN busy every day since last week. The chicken pox had run its course through the small town. He was sure every child under twelve had been exposed. Things had started slowing down, until a wave of mono hit the High School.

His office was no longer filled with crying itchy children, but filled instead with coughing, moody teenagers. He preferred the small children.

He really hated canceling lunch with Lacey, since it was his one chance to break free from a normally mundane day. Things had never looked better in his life. His parents had not only shown respect for his decision to move to Pride, but since the Jennifer incident, he had actually felt like they had connected for the first time.

His relationship with Lacey was mended. His parents hadn't really commented on it, but after Jennifer, he got the feeling they preferred to keep out of his love life.

He was filling out what felt like the hundredth prescription for the day, when Betty came running in.

"There's been an accident out front. Hurry!" He'd never seen the old lady move so fast she ran into the front office. "I'm calling an ambulance," she said without looking up at him.

By the time he ran out into the rain, there were several

people gathered around, all holding umbrellas over the small figure that sat on the curb, cradling her left arm. When he reached the small body, his mind shut off.

Her purple rain coat was torn, as were her pants and shirt. There were scratches on her knees and arms.

Lacey looked up into his eyes and everything switched off. None of his medical training had ever prepared him for this.

"The car just came out of nowhere. I swear it aimed right at her; it didn't even stop. Who would do that?" Betty said, now standing behind him. She handed him his medical bag. He bent down over Lacey and got to work cleaning her wounds.

His hands shook when they reached for her, but his mind finally clicked on and his instincts had taken over. But when they reached the hospital, he could no longer mask the fear in his eyes. She was scratched and bloody, and would no doubt have many bruises, and possibly a broken arm, but he hadn't heard one complaint from her.

Once the ambulance had reached the hospital in Edgeview, Dr. Berger had taken over, leaving Aaron to wait in the room with the rest of her family.

Aaron had met Dr. Berger on many occasions; he liked the man, and he trusted him. Now, however, as he sat in a small room packed with Lacey's family and some of the town people, he wanted nothing more than to waltz back into the examining room and take over.

Just as he stood to do so, the doctor walked out.

They all walked forward to hear what he had to say, Todd signing for Iian as the doctor started talked.

"She just has a slight concussion and a sprained wrist, but I want to keep her overnight. They're checking her into a room now." Aaron looked down the hall to see her being pushed in a bed towards the elevators.

Just then his phone rang, and he stepped away for a minute to take the call from his grandfather.

A few minutes later the three men and Megan walked into her room. Aaron was the last one in and stood in the very back.

Her brother Todd spoke first, "Hi, sugar." He tried to smile at her. Megan was holding Matthew close and Lacey could see quiet tears roll down her face.

Iian came over and held her hand that wasn't wrapped in a tight splint. Instead of signing, he spoke.

"How's my big sis?" His voice was like water in the desert.

"I've been better. Aaron?" She looked at him standing in the corner. His eyes were red and had something close to panic in them.

"What is it Aaron? What's wrong?" He stepped forward and everyone in the room looked at him.

"I just got off the phone with my grandfather. The Sheriff talked to Betty, and well..." He walked around, pulling his hands through his hair, wanting to pull it out. "It's all my fault."

Everyone continued to look at him, no one said anything.

He continued, "It was Jennifer. Jennifer was behind the wheel. She did this, almost killed Lacey, because of me. It's my fault. I should have been..."

"Stop it!" Megan stepped forward, holding little Matthew close. When Aaron started to speak, she interrupted. "No, you'll listen to me for a while."

She gently handed Matthew to her husband. "For years I blamed myself for the hell I went through. I told myself it was my fault -- the fights, the bruises, broken bones, and all that pain. But then I woke up one day, I think it was another one of my many hospital visits, and I just knew that no matter how hard I tried, I couldn't justify what had happened to me. There was nothing I could have done to make Derek's crazy go away. I was not to blame for anything he did to me or the craziness he had. Just like now, there was nothing you could have done to prevent what Jennifer did. Nothing!"

Walking over to Lacey, Megan took her bandaged hand in her own. "If I know anything about you -- and I think I do -- I know you would never blame Aaron for this."

"Of course not! I agree. Aaron, there was nothing you could have done." He walked over and took Lacey's hand from her brother, who quietly stepped back.

"If I had just…" he started to say.

"Shhh." Looking up into Todd's eyes, she pleaded with him.

"We're just going to take a walk." Todd walked to the door holding Matthew. Megan and Iian quietly followed him out. When the door shut with a light click, Lacey continued.

"You know how much you mean to me. I have never and would never blame you for…"

Aaron leaned over and kissed her lips, quieting her with his mouth.

"I don't want to lose you, I can't lose you. Stay with me, be with me." He leaned his forehead against hers. "Be with me, forever." She pulled back and looked at him, understanding.

"Are you sure? Because I don't play games, Aaron. If I say yes, I come with a family, a town, a dog, the whole nine yards." She looked into his eyes. "I don't want to move to the east coast, California, or…"

His mouth covered hers again. "I want all of that Lacey. All of it! If it comes with you. What do you say? Please say yes?"

Looking deeply into his eyes, she saw the truth. "Of course, yes." She smiled and was kissed again.

TO LACEY the hospital seemed like a three-ring circus. She had spent Valentines night in a bright room, being woken up and checked what seemed like every five minutes. Aaron sat in the chair next to her bed, sleeping in between nurse visits. He watched over everything they did and even double checked everything again after they left. After successfully making it through the night without killing anyone out of frustration, she was released, and sent home.

A few hours later she sat propped up at Aaron's house. She had a dozen or so townspeople around her chatting and eating the food that everyone had brought. Aaron announced their engagement shortly after arriving home. The news was followed with cheers.

It was a tradition that the town people came out in spades when one of their own was hurt. She had been there for others in town. When Betty had lost her husband, when Tom and Becca had been married, when Matt had died, she had been there for everyone. She had also been there when Megan had been recovering from the explosion that was her ex-husband.

Now everyone was here for her. She was propped up on the couch, her left arm tucked close and wrapped tight in a splint, her cuts all bandaged. Her bruises were beginning to turn a darker purple, and the Motrin she had taken earlier was starting to wear off. But still she smiled and chatted as best she could. She was finding it hard to concentrate on conversations, but these were her people and they had come out for her, to show her how much they cared, how much they loved her.

She was on orders from her doctor to rest for the next week, a doctor who was standing across the room helping dish out some of Betty's wonderful angel food cake. It had snowed again last night, and to her it seemed that spring was years away. She enjoyed the snow, she even enjoyed being out in it, but just now, she wished for the warmer rains of spring.

Aaron watched her from across the room. She was pale, bruised, cut, and could have ended up dead, all because of him. Oh, he heard everything Megan had said yesterday, but to be honest, he kept playing everything over and over in his mind.

If he had just handled Jennifer differently, maybe, just maybe, he could have gotten through to her. Thinking of what could have happened to Lacey, his mind fogged. Lacey. Sweet, trusting Lacey.

Thinking of the differences between the two women, there was no doubt about Lacey's honesty. He had never really trusted Jennifer. It had always been something else: desire. He had wanted something he had never had before, and he thought he would have it with Jennifer. A family. Now, however, when he looked around his crowded living room, he realized this was what he had always thought the true meaning of "family" was.

LACEY WAS BORED after three days of doing nothing. Did Aaron really believe she needed this much time to recover from a few scratches and a twisted wrist? She was determined to tell him so, just as soon as he got home. She was going to work tomorrow, and she didn't care whether he had lots of fancy degrees and years of medical school. She was feeling well enough to go to work. She would lay off carrying heavy trays of food for a while, but at least she could do simple things. The sitting around was driving her nuts.

Aaron had stayed home that first day after the accident, but then he had gone off to work and left her there alone. Watching daytime TV was only fun if you had someone to watch with. Besides, she had never really gotten into the whole soap opera scene, and she didn't think she wanted to start.

Iian, Todd and Megan visited on and off, but for the most part, she was on her own, at least until she could convince her doctor to prescribe a good dose of work.

At least Bernard and Cleo had been keeping her company. They were running through the back yard, playing in the snow, when she heard a car drive up.

———

IT HAD TAKEN ONLY three days of staying in the slimy motel outside of Edgeview to make up her mind. She wasn't about to lose. The man at the motel believed her when she said her fiancée had abandoned her there with no money, just the rental car. She even told him that she was waiting for her sister to bring her money and that the bill would be paid in full on Friday. She had no intention of paying or going back to the filthy dive.

What she did have in mind was getting rid of the bitch that had ruined everything. She had even driven to the hospital and pretended to be concerned but hadn't gotten any updates on Lacey's health. Bruises and scratches did nothing to clear the path for her; she needed more action. Something more permanent. Now, after days of planning it, she knew exactly what to do.

Knocking on Aaron's door, she started to shake, knowing this should be her door, her house with Aaron. They could have children here, or maybe they could move back east, get that place in the gated community. Yes, she would show Aaron that it would be for the best, to move away from the backwater hellhole, he'd been hiding in.

When the slut answered the door, it was so easy. She was

so small; one swing had her sprawled on the floor in a small little heap.

KNOWING IT WAS IMPORTANT, Lacey tried to stay focused. Her head hurt, and she had landed on her bad wrist. Looking up from the ground, she saw Jennifer step in and shut the door. Pushing up from the ground, she kicked out, catching Jennifer in the knee. When Jennifer fell, Lacey got up and made it past the front porch before her bad arm was wrenched behind her.

"Now, let's try this again, shall we?" Lacey felt the blade on her neck, then she heard the dogs barking.

"What the…" Jennifer backed up, pulling Lacey with her. "Call them off now," she said as the two dogs came running around the corner. Bernard was growling and baring his teeth. When Cleo felt his tension, she piped in with her own low growls.

Lacey tried to think. "Bernard, go to Megan's." She said in a shaky voice. Knowing Cleo would follow him, she sent them to the only place she knew help would be.

As Bernard continued to growl, Lacey said it again in a more forceful voice. This time he stopped, looked at her, then turned and ran down the path, with Cleo trailing behind him slowly.

"What do you want, Jennifer?" She tried to sound calm and tried to think.

"I want Aaron, he's mine. He just needs to get all the distractions out of the way. I just need to clear the way, and then he'll see that he can't live without me."

Lacey could see Jennifer's eyes darting around, looking for an escape route. As Jennifer started pulling her down the path towards the pond, Lacey knew she was in trouble.

Jennifer was yanking her arm up behind her back, causing searing pain.

"There is only so much I can tolerate, I mean, seriously. Do you think Aaron would hang around here much longer? You know the life, the family he came from. They're above all this, this backwater life you live. Seriously, can you imagine him living here? In this dirty place?" She stumbled on a tree root jutting from the ground. "I mean there's only so much filth I can put up with."

Jennifer was marching fast enough down the path, that Lacey was being dragged. Her arm throbbed, her head was splitting, and she was starting to see double.

They reached the clearing just as snow flakes started to fall in wet clumps. When Jennifer saw the pond, she dragged Lacey to the large rock that hung over the frozen water.

Lacey fought, she kicked, dragged her feet, did everything she could, until Jennifer nicked her neck with the knife and tightened her hold. She was shivering now. She had no shoes, no jacket. All she was wearing was light sweat pants, a light t-shirt, and her Bert and Ernie socks.

When they got to the pond, Lacey realized she was out of options. They stood at the water's edge as flakes clung to Lacey's eyelashes and hair. Then, she heard the dogs barking, and the sweetest sound on the earth followed. She heard Aaron calling her name.

———

TODD AND IIAN were heading over to see their sister, to deliver a stack of books that she had requested. When they rounded the corner to go up the drive, they saw Aaron's truck turning in before them. Waving to him, they followed him up the long drive.

Just as they reached the house, they noticed the silver

sedan. Both men jumped out of the car before Todd had put it in park.

"What the hell?" Aaron slammed his truck door shut and raced to the opened front door, yelling for Lacey.

Iian noticed it first. Bending down in the doorway, he saw the blood, and yelled for the other two men.

Just as Aaron reached the doorway again, Bernard came running up, shaking, and barking. When Todd reached down to grab his collar, he noticed blood on his nose, lots of blood.

"Damn it, where the hell is she? Bernard, where is Lacey?" Aaron said, stepping out on the porch, looking frantically around.

Iian bent down and grabbed Bernard by the collar. "Find Lacey," he said and snapped his fingers.

Bernard took one look at the trio, barked and then ran down the path towards his master.

Sprinting ahead of the other two, Aaron could see Bernard cut to the left, heading towards the pond.

"The pond," he yelled out for Todd and knew Iian would follow.

When Aaron reached the edge of the clearing, he saw Lacey and Jennifer standing on the large rock near the water.

Jennifer held a knife pointed at Lacey's heart.

Just then, Jennifer swung her arm up, and Aaron saw the knife arc downwards.

He screamed.

Lacey stepped backwards just as Bernard lunged at Jennifer. Bernard's teeth sunk deep into Jennifer's arm, the knife digging deep into Bernard's fur.

Lacey's socked feet slipped on the icy rock, her head hit the edge, and then she fell into the cold water and sunk below its dark surface.

Just for a minute, he thought he might be fast enough to reach the edge of the pond to catch her before she went in.

As he ran to the water's edge, he saw a brown spot rush past him, going straight into the water after Lacey. Bernard had Jennifer on her knees, her arm firmly gripped between his teeth. She dropped the knife, as he continued to yank on her arm. Blood dripped from Bernard's shoulder, but the dog didn't pay any attention.

When Aaron pushed past them, he could see the crack in the ice where Lacey and Cleo had disappeared. Not even giving Jennifer a thought, he leaped into the pond, just as Cleo was coming back up for air. The small dog paddled around barking, then dove back under the cold water and followed Aaron on his search.

The water was cold, freezing cold. He had to find her! Using all his strength, he reached out, looking, feeling his way around the dark pond. Where was she?

LACEY WAS FLOATING, drifting in a weightless dream as white puffy clouds floated above her head. She could hear the dogs playing near the shore through the soft lapping sound of the water. It tickled her sides as she floated, cooling her hot skin.

Then she could hear someone calling her name. She tried to open her eyes, but something was pulling her back into the darkness. She hurt, and the darkness provided a reprieve from the pain. She thought about floating for a while longer.

HE FELT something brush against his foot. Reaching down, he felt fur. Cleo. Letting her go, he continued his search, reaching and searching.

He searched until his lungs screamed, then he surfaced to gulp in a desperately needed breath.

Iian had Jennifer held down, the knife held tightly in his hand. He was yelling for Lacey, screaming her name. Todd had jumped in the pond shortly after Aaron had.

Diving under again, Aaron continued to search for what seemed like hours. Again, he ran into Cleo, but this time the small dog had something in her mouth and was trying to get to the surface. Grabbing hold, Aaron rushed the two upwards.

LACEY COULD SEE colors and hear voices and she felt hands touching her. She heard a baby cry and more voices. She felt herself being lifted and rearranged. Then she felt warm liquid in her arms, warming her entire body. She couldn't stop shaking. Why couldn't she stop shaking?

Then it was quiet, so quiet. She opened her eyes and stared at a white ceiling. She felt dull, her eyes had a hard time focusing and she blinked a few times to clear her mind. She couldn't remember where she was or how she'd gotten there. She just hoped it wasn't the hospital again!

Everything was a little too blurry for her to see clearly. Then he leaned over her and her eyes focused on him and nothing else mattered.

EPILOGUE

*L*acey was floating again. This time, the cool water was a welcome reprieve from the scorching heat.

Bernard and Cleo, her heroes, were both happily barking and splashing around, making waves in the cool water. Bernard had had his stitches removed and had been given a clean bill of health.

It had taken a few weeks for her to get back on her feet after the last dip she'd taken in this pond. Blocking the memory from her thoughts, she continued to look up into the blue sky and watch what few clouds were there.

By this time next month, she would be Mrs. Aaron Stevens. Smiling now to herself, she could just see it; walking down the aisle in her church, Aaron standing there with Father Michael and her brothers, the whole town of Pride there to celebrate. Of course, there would be a party afterward at the restaurant, where all of Pride and her family would join in the celebration.

Hearing a splash, she looked over towards the shore just in time to see a large wave. Knowing what was coming next, she quickly ducked under to play a quick game of cat and mouse with her soon-to-be husband. Just who was the cat, and who was the mouse, had yet to be decided. But she knew they would both enjoy discovering the answer, together.

PREVIEW OF RETURNING PRIDE

*O*verlooking the water, Iian watched as the waves crashed violently on the rocks below the cliffs. Winter was almost over, yet the cold seemed to hang in the air. Low dark clouds hovered over the dark horizon as mist clung all around him. The rain had stopped an hour earlier, leaving a lingering scent in the breeze that hit his face. This was his home; he belonged here and just knew it. He could see the lights from fishing boats, they were scattered along the shoreline. Though unable to hear, he knew fog horns would be sounding, signaling their warning of the jagged shore.

It had been over ten years since his accident, which had left him without his father, and without his hearing. The nightmares of that day still haunted him. He couldn't remember all the details, but his memories played like a broken record in his head.

It took him almost a year to get over his physical wounds. Learning a new language had been hard for him, even harder on his brother and sister, Todd and Lacey. Sign language was now something he did without thinking. The pain of losing their father, however, had taken a lot longer for them to get over.

Their father had been the glue that had held their family together, after the loss of their mother at Iian's birth. His father had worked hard at the restaurant that had been his parents' dream, making enough to start his own business, Jordan Shipping, which Iian's brother Todd now ran. After their father's death, his sister Lacey had stepped in and taken over the role of holding everyone together.

After losing his hearing, Iian started noticing a few things happening to him. He noticed his eyesight, his sense of smell, and his taste had sharpened immensely. These enhancements had helped with his career as a chef but lowered his ability to deal with other people.

He knew what everyone saw in him. He was tall, standing a little over six-and-a-half feet. He had been rail thin until about the ninth grade, when he'd hit his last growing spurt. He worked out regularly and since his youth had added to his bulk with lean muscles, which he was proud of. His dark hair and light crystal eyes were a family trait, as well as the small cleft in his chin.

As he pushed his hair out of his eyes, he stood on the small cliff and looked around. To his left, columns of smoke rose from houses in the small tight-knit community of Pride, Oregon. He could just make out the green roof of The Golden Oar, his restaurant, his life. The larger, old building sat on the waterfront, just off the main street in town. The place had been his sole focus since his accident. He'd been raised working in the kitchen or the dining halls, it had been in his blood. Handed down from several generations, now the place was his, coming to him on his twenty-fifth birthday. It was a good thing that cooking was in his blood, it just happened to be a bonus that it was his passion as well.

He could think of only one other thing he'd felt this way

about, and he was wondering when she'd come back into town.

ALLISON WAS HOME, there was no doubt about it. She'd missed the old place; it had never looked so inviting. The house was dark except for the tall lamps on either side of the cement path that lead to the bright blue front door. The cool evening rain was washing the sidewalk and streets, making them shine and look new.

She remembered when her father was alive, the house had been in pristine shape. Shortly after his death, money was short and they had a harder time taking care of everything. Well, the house had been the last thing on their minds then.

The blue shutters on the windows still hung strong, they just needed some paint. Actually, the whole house could use a fresh coat, for that matter. The inside had always been kept in tip-top shape. Her mother had always been somewhat of a perfectionist, especially when it came to her house.

Thinking of her mother, she turned off her car and realized that she'd always had more of a partnership rather than a mother-daughter relationship. Especially after her sister, Abby, had died.

Taking a deep breath, she opened her car door and made a run for the front door through the pouring rain, her keys and overnight bag on-hand.

She had expected her mother to be asleep at this late hour; she'd left Los Angeles a little later than planned due to traffic, which had slowed her trip by a good two hours.

When she opened the front door, she had to jerk it open. She turned on the lights and what she found scared her. One of the couch cushions was on the floor; there was a large pile of dirty clothes in the corner by the television set, which was still on. There were dishes sitting on the coffee table that looked like they'd been there for weeks. Turning on lights, she ran into the back and was even more shocked by what she saw the kitchen. Something was definitely not right! Things were thrown around in there as well. Rushing to the back of the small house, she knocked on her mother's door as she pushed it open.

"Mom? Can I come in? Mom, is everything okay?" She shoved the door, pushing clothes that had piled up behind it.

Allison saw a small lump in the bed and quickly switched on the light. Her mother's face was pale and thin. She must have lost at least ten pounds since she'd seen her around six months ago. Her curly, black hair was streaked with silver and stuck straight up, giving her an *"I've just seen a ghost,"* look. It was her mother's eyes that worried her the most. They were red-rimmed and staring blankly and looked completely empty as her mother looked at her. Teresa Adams was in her mid-sixties and had been alone for almost a third of her life.

"Abby. Oh, your back! Did you forget your umbrella?" She attempted to sit up in bed.

"No Mama, it's me, Allison," Allison sat next to her mother and felt her forehead, checking for a fever. Her mother's head was hot, and she could see her was shaking with a fever.

"Oh, I'm sorry dear. Mommy was just taking a quick nap and you know how your father gets when you forget your umbrella. Better run and get it or you'll be late for school." Teresa started to lie back down.

"Oh, Mom," Allison leaned over. Picking up the phone, she dialed the local doctor's number from memory.

"Hello?" The voice sounded younger than the eighty-year-old man who was the normal doctor in town.

"I... I'm sorry, I think I have the wrong number," she started to hang up.

"This is Dr. Stevens. Are you looking for a doctor?"

"Yes, this is Allison Adams. My mother is running a high fever and she isn't coherent. Can you come quickly?"

"Yes, Miss Adams, I can be there in about ten minutes."

"Thank you," Allison hung up and went into the adjoining bath to get a cold cloth for her mother.

AARON WATCHED AS HIS WIFE, Lacey, rolled over and asked, "Mrs. Adams? Is something wrong?"

"She's running a fever, her daughter called. It shouldn't take me long to deal with this. Go back to bed." He looked over at his wife, as he pulled on a pair of worn jeans and a warm sweater.

It had been three years since he'd taken over his grandfather's medical practice in Pride. Two years since his marriage to the woman who now carried their first child. He smiled down at her small form in the bed.

"Allison called? I didn't know she was back in town," Lacey said slowly sitting up. "I should go with you, see if there's something I can do," she started to rise.

"Oh, no you don't," he rushed over to place his hands on her shoulders. "If you start going on all my house calls, who's going to stay home and take care of our children?" He smiled down at her glowing face and gently laid a hand on her small, but growing belly. "Besides, it's wet and cold out there. You should keep my side of the bed warm for when I come back." He leaned over and kissed her. "I should be back soon."

He was gone before she could say another word. When exactly had she lost control? Oh yeah, the day she'd bumped into him. She smiled into the pillow and remembered that wonderful hot day and quickly fell back asleep.

ALLISON HAD TURNED on every light while she waited for the doctor. She had just started to clean the front room when there was a quick knock on the door. She rushed over and opened the door quickly for the doctor.

"Thank God. She's just back--" she dropped off as a very tall, very wet male started to step into the light.

Taking a large step back she grabbed the only thing handy, one of her mother's favorite crystal candle sticks.

"Who are you?" She demanded holding the candle stick like a batter ready to hit a home run.

"Allison, it's me, Aaron Stevens, remember we met before," he stepped into the doorway farther, the light finally hit his face. "You were expecting my grandfather, remember, he retired," he smiled down at her. "I'd hate to go back to my wife and explain why I have stitches in my head," he said holding out his hands.

Then she remembered that he'd married Lacey. She'd even attended their wedding when they'd been married on the beach a few years back. It must be that she was tired from the long trip and maybe the worry of her mother was warping her brain. Quickly setting down her weapon, she wiped her sweaty hands on her jeans.

"Oh my god! I'm so sorry, it slipped my mind. I just drove several hours and my brain isn't in gear. Come in, my mother's in the back." She pointed him towards the back and started walking to her mother's room.

He followed her, walking past the messy front room. She noticed that he took a quick look around.

"I just got home tonight. It appears she's been sick for a while." She waved a hand at the disarray.

When they reached her mother's bedroom, Aaron got to work.

"Are you just visiting from California?" he asked, while checking her mother's blood pressure.

"Yes! No! I was planning on staying, I don't know yet. I just decided to come back last week; something just called me home." How could she explain that she'd felt drawn home? That she'd felt like she'd been starved in the city. "Is she going to be okay?" She asked, she knew she had a worried look on her face as she was nervously fidgeting with her hands.

"Well, to be honest, I don't like your mother's blood pressure, and her temperature really worries me. I'd like to run some more tests." He set his stethoscope down and leaned over to check the dilation of her pupils. Leaning back up he looked at her.

"Allison, I'd like to move your mother to the hospital in Edgeview. I can have an ambulance come pick her up," He said, as her mother started to mumble and toss about.

"Yes, of course," she said, focusing on her mother's face.

"I'll just step out and make the call." Aaron walked into the living room.

Less than an hour later, when the paramedics wheeled her mother into the emergency room, Allison and Aaron were right on their heels. She saw Lacey waiting just inside the front door of the hospital. She rushed over and gave her friend a big hug, bumping lightly into her small, pregnant belly.

"It's so good to have you back," Lacey smiled at Allison. "How is she?" she asked as she turned to her husband.

"I'm going to go find out. I'll be back shortly." He gave Lacey's hand a squeeze and disappeared down the hall where they had wheeled Allison's mom.

The two women walked up to the front nurse's desk and signed in. Lacey talked to the nurse briefly, then they turned to go sit in the waiting area, which was almost empty. The two television sets were set to the same news channel, and there was an older couple sitting across the way watching the weather.

Edgeview Medical Center was the only facility within fifty miles, so naturally, sometimes it was quite full. During the short trip there, Dr. Stevens, Aaron, he'd wanted her to call him, told her he had taken over his grandfather's local office in Pride. But he confirmed that it was more for appointments and not emergencies such as this. Here, they could run blood work, do x-rays, even surgery if needed. Her mind numbed at that thought.

Lacey had stopped at the vending machines and grabbed a bottled of water for each of them. "Come and sit down. Aaron will take care of your mother," she said, taking a quick sip of her water. "I didn't know you were back in town."

"I… I just got in about an hour ago. The place was messy; you know how my mom is about everything being tidy." Lacey shook her head, "I don't even know how long she'd been sick? If I hadn't gotten home tonight…"

Lacey took a good look at her; and Allison knew what she was seeing. She was a lot thinner than the last time Lacey had seen her. Her eyes felt dull and Ally felt like she needed a good night's sleep.

"You must be tired after the long drive. Why don't you try to stretch out on the couch?" Lacey patted the cushions next to her. How could she refuse? Lacey had babysat Allison and Abby a lot when they were younger. She'd been like a really cool older sister to the pair.

Resting her head back on the small couch, she realized that she was very tired, but didn't think she could fall asleep. Her mind kept going back to what she had seen at the house, how her mother had looked lost.

Even with the hum of the television, the bright lights, and the worry on her mind, she still drifted off. A few hours later, she was awakened by Dr. Stevens, who informed her they had moved her mother into a private room on the second floor. She was stable, but her fever was still holding. He told her they were running several tests and wouldn't know the results until morning.

When Allison was finally allowed to see her mother half an hour later, she walked into the room with Lacey trailing behind her. Allison was grateful for the support of her friend.

She sat in the chair closest to her mother. Aaron pulled his wife aside and had a quiet conversation with her, after which she announced that she was heading home and would be back first thing in the morning.

Then he stood next to the bed and checking the IV tubes.

"What can you tell me?"

"Not much more tonight. I'm waiting for the lab results. It shouldn't be much longer." He looked at his watch, "I'll just go check on them."

He turned and left Alison in a room with the bright lights, loud machines, and her mother laying there, drugged and sleeping.

ALSO BY JILL SANDERS

The Pride Series
Finding Pride
Discovering Pride
Returning Pride
Lasting Pride
Serving Pride
Red Hot Christmas
My Sweet Valentine
Return To Me
Rescue Me

The Secret Series
Secret Seduction
Secret Pleasure
Secret Guardian
Secret Passions
Secret Identity
Secret Sauce

The West Series

Loving Lauren
Taming Alex
Holding Haley
Missy's Moment
Breaking Travis
Roping Ryan
Wild Bride
Corey's Catch
Tessa's Turn

The Grayton Series
Last Resort
Someday Beach
Rip Current
In Too Deep
Swept Away
High Tide

Lucky Series
Unlucky In Love
Sweet Resolve
Best of Luck
A Little Luck

Silver Cove Series
Silver Lining
French Kiss
Happy Accident
Hidden Charm
A Silver Cove Christmas

Entangled Series – Paranormal Romance
The Awakening
The Beckoning

The Ascension

St. Helena Vineyard Kindle Worlds
Where I Belong

Haven, Montana Series
Closer to You
Never Let Go
Holding On

Pride Oregon Series
A Dash of Love
My Kind of Love
For a complete list of books: http://JillSanders.com

ABOUT THE AUTHOR

Jill Sanders is *The New York Times* and *USA Today* bestselling author of Sweet Small-Town Contemporary Romance Series, Thrilling Romantic Suspense Series, Sexy Western Romance Series, and Intriguing Paranormal Romance novels. She continues to lure new readers with her sweet and sexy stories. Her books are available in every English-speaking country and in audiobooks as well as being translated into different languages.

Born as an identical twin to a large family, she was raised in the Pacific Northwest and later relocated to Colorado for college and a successful IT career before discovering her talent as a writer. She now makes her home along the Emerald Coast in Florida where she enjoys the beach, hiking, swimming, wine-tasting, and of course writing.

Connect on http://fb.com/JillSandersBooks
    Twitter: https://twitter.com/JillMSanders
    Website: http://JillSanders.com

Printed in Great Britain
by Amazon